The Beauty
&
The Blonde

D A Latham

ISBN:-10 1483911217
ISBN-13:978-1483911212

DEDICATION

To my dearest, darling Allan.

CONTENTS

The Beauty & The Blonde

ACKNOWLEDGMENTS

With thanks to Christina Pettitt for all her help and good advice.

CHAPTER 1

"Looking good Dionne," said Louise, Dionne's hairdresser as she added the finishing touches to her shiny, blonde hair. The makeup artist had already packed up and left, so all Dionne had to do was get dressed and she was ready to go. She stared at herself in the large mirror of her dressing table, and gave herself a pep talk.

'You can do this, a night out will do you good' she told herself.

Tonight was drinks at Claridges, then dinner at Gordon Ramsey's restaurant. Lynne, Dionne's best friend had heard the menu had changed there, and really wanted to try it out. Dionne would rather have stayed home and worked, but thankfully Lynne was around to make sure she didn't.

Lynne breezed through the door carrying two glasses of wine. "Love your hair, makeup looks good too. Are we out on the pull then tonight?" She winked playfully.

"Me? On the pull? Think those days are over" said Dionne sadly, taking a gulp of her wine.

"It's been two years now Di," said Lynne."John wouldn't have wanted you to lock yourself away and spend your life in front of a computer, he wanted you to be happy, and he would have wanted you to be loved too."

Dionne sighed. She knew Lynne was right, but the thought of dating, or more, with anyone else was terrifying. After 18 years of happy marriage, it would take a bloody big deep breath to get close to another man.

She was content with her life as it was. After John's death, she threw herself into work, charity functions, and her friends. Between them, they kept her busy, tired and sane. She couldn't imagine sharing her life with another man, if there was a man who wanted her.

'Ok John, if there's someone out there, send him to me,' she thought.

Lynne had laid out her outfit ready for Dionne to get dressed. Lynne had serious fashion talent, and had been shopping for Dionne long enough to know exactly what would fit and suit Dionne's tiny frame. Tonight she had laid out a cream Dior dress, subtly embellished with embroidery, and very fitted to show off a tiny waist and slim figure. She had added cream kitten heel Jimmy Choo's, and some pearl jewellery that she had found digging around in Dionne's jewellery room.

The two women had been friends since school. Their friendship had endured right through Dionne's marriage and when John died of a heart attack age 42, both of them had grieved.

They had found a formula that worked for them. Dionne loved working in finance, and Lynne loved spending money. Dionne converted some mews houses at the back of her mansion for Lynne so she could live 'next door', and gave her a black Amex.

Lynne ensured that Dionne always had outfits, functions to attend, and beauty treatments scheduled as required. In short, Lynne kept her looking presentable and stopped her working 18 hour days every day.

Once Dionne was dressed, the pair of them finished their wine, and made their way out to the Bentley waiting on the drive. Joe, Dionne's driver tipped his hat and held the door open for Dionne, while Craig,(their bodyguard) held the door open for Lynne. Craig slid into the seat next to Joe, and they set off for Mayfair.

The bar at Claridges was busy and buzzy. It was a fairly small bar, but tended to be fairly exclusive, and served the best G&T's in London.

"The beautiful people are out in force tonight," mused Dionne. They both ordered gin and tonics, and settled into their seats to peruse the room.

"Dionne! How lovely to see you" called out a rather ugly, squat, man walking towards them smiling, with an Amazonian blonde on his arm."Let me introduce my new girlfriend Lieka," he smiled.

"Douggie! How the devil are you?" Said Dionne, smiling widely. "Are you being a dirty old rogue with this pretty young thing?" She asked quietly while he kissed both her cheeks.

"It's ok Di, she doesn't speak a word of English, which suits me perfectly," he winked at her.

Lynne smirked at Dionne. "Wonder how much he paid for her," she whispered.

"Can we meet up next week Di? I need to talk to you about that Scottish land deal" said Douggie, suddenly serious.

"Sure, can you give my PA a call and fix a day and time?" replied Dionne, wondering why he wanted a face to face. Land deals could generally be done over the phone.

"Will do. Well we better be finding our table. Quicker we eat the quicker I can get Lieka home" he smirked, and patted her bum. Lynne thought she caught a look of revulsion on Lieka's face, but within a second it was gone, an impassive smile taking its place.

"That is my problem with men our age," mused Dionne, "they are all a bit, well, slaggy, and would rather buy a bimbo off the net than have a proper partner. The decent ones are married, and younger men are gonna be either intimidated or gold digging."

"Hmm," agreed Lynne absent-mindedly, too busy eyeing up a small group of men at the bar. "They look familiar over there, do we know them?

Dionne craned her neck slightly to see. "No, don't think so, nice looking though," one in particular catching her eye. *'What a beautiful man'* she thought.

At that moment, a smartly dressed older man walked into the bar, saw the group and headed over to join them. After some hellos, he scanned the room, alighting his gaze on Dionne and Lynne. Smiling widely he excused himself and came over.

"Dionne, Lynne, how lovely to see you both, are you out for dinner?" Dionne stood up to greet him, and he wrapped his arms round her in a hug. Holding her at arms length to look at her, he smiled appraisingly."Looking ravishing as always."

"Ralph, it's wonderful to see you, yes, Lynne and I are here to try the new menu. Are you eating, or just here for a drink?"

"Celebrating tonight Di," said Ralph. "Brought some of my artists out for a celebratory dinner. Those strings you pulled for me sure paid off. All four of them have decent roles lined up, and two have just been paid from their last movie roles. That means I just got paid too."

Ralph was an agent. He owned Celebrity Artists inc. Good at his job, he had the hottest stars on his books. Dionne and John had invested at the start to get him going, plus they owned the building he operated from. Of course now it was just Dionne. What she didn't broadcast was her share holdings in all the major Hollywood studios. She held those shares in one of many anonymous and convoluted holding companies. It meant she could network and subtly influence without pesky journalists or nosy parkers being able to link all her shareholdings, and publish her wealth on the Forbes list.

After kissing Lynne on both cheeks, Ralph invited the two ladies to join them for dinner. After checking with the maitre'd, they made their way over to the bar to be introduced to the people they would be dining with.

"This is Ian, Josh, Daniel and Harry" said Ralph. Harry gave Dionne his best knicker combusting smile. *'What a truly perfect young man,'* thought Dionne, beaming back. Each of the young men shook hands with the two women. " and this is Dionne and Lynne, great friends of mine who will be joining us tonight," said Ralph. The young men all smiled bar Harry, who's smile had quickly faded.

Dionne guessed that Ian and Josh were mid twenties, with Daniel and Harry nearer 30. All of them were drop dead gorgeous in slightly different ways. Not one of them would have warranted kicking out of bed. Lynne was in seventh heaven having four beautiful young men to entertain through dinner.

Lynne beamed. This evening was turning out better than hoped. She was a gregarious and good looking blonde. Tall and slim, she had never lacked male attention, just never 'the one'. The rather sad truth was that she was picky in the extreme to mask a serious issue with commitment.

They were shown to a large circular table in the centre of the restaurant. Dionne was seated between Ralph and Harry, while Lynne sat between Daniel and Ian. Josh sat between Ian and Ralph. They all decided to have the rather interesting tasting menu rather than try and decipher the rather daunting a la carte menu.

Ralph ordered a bottle of Krug, and raised a toast "To the continued success of Celebrity Artists." They all clinked glasses and drank.

Turning to her left, Dionne asked Harry, "So what film have you just wrapped?"

Harry looked a bit pained, but answered "Ulysses, it's a myth and legend type film," in a sulky voice as if he didn't want to be there talking to her. Dionne frowned slightly. He hadn't looked bored or pained before at the bar, he had looked happy and animated.

'Maybe it was the company of women?' She decided that he was probably gay. Men that good looking usually were. Gay men didn't usually sulk at having to talk to women though.

Harry had clocked Dionne the moment she had walked in. She really was just his type. Dainty, with glossy blonde hair, big blue eyes and a soft, sensual mouth, he had really struggled not to stare at her. He would never had tried to start a conversation with her, as he was too racked with self doubt. He was shy around women he fancied, not that he would like to admit it, as it was a bit at odds with the whole movie star persona, plus, he rarely came across a woman he truly found attractive.

6

He went from being delighted at being introduced, to mortified that he was expected to sit next to her and make conversation for an entire evening. He worried that once he had used up the characters he had played in films as conversation, he would be completely stuck on what to say, and she would realise he was boring and gauche. Sadly an all boy household, an all male education, and working on male dominated action films had left him lacking the ability to chat effortlessly with the opposite sex. So he sat there tongue tied, unfortunately looking bored and rather miserable.

'Oh god, she's exquisite, I wish I could sweep her off her feet and kiss her all over. She smells divine. Wonder what her tits are like' he thought, as he struggled not to stare.

Dionne sat wondering what was wrong with him. She decided to try and make conversation."So where are you from Harry?"

He turned to reply, "Southampton", and as soon as he looked at her, she noticed his pupils dilate.

Dionne was pretty observant and wasn't ignorant of human nature. She was picking up his reactions, analysing them, and reading him. She figured he had issues with women. So she countered it by being friendly, humorous and chatty, coaxing him out of his shell.

Harry concentrated on listening to her voice, he was mesmerised by her soft, girlish giggle, and gentle London accent, deducing correctly that she hadn't attended public school like he had. Despite her lack of aristocratic roots, Harry thought she was the most charismatic woman he had ever met. He was totally transfixed.

Lynne was thoroughly enjoying the two young men vying for her attention through dinner. She had an easy way with her which made people relax.

Observing the laughter across the table, Harry touched Dionne's arm, "your friend seems to be having a good time."

"She's great fun, and she adores the company of men, so a film star

7

sandwich is her idea of heaven," Dionne replied with a smile.

"Do you like younger men?" Asked Harry, feeling brave, and desperate to pick up any clues that she might be remotely interested in him.

"I don't really know to be honest, I was married for a long time, so didn't really have to worry about flirting and all that sort of stuff."

Harry blinked. "Was married? What happened?" Then regretted being nosy, worrying that he had asked the wrong question.

"My husband died a couple of years ago. Very sudden" Dionne said softly, twigging that he was embarrassed that he had asked.

To lighten things up, Dionne whispered to Harry, "quick, wig at ten o clock!" Harry looked over to see who Dionne was talking about. The man in question was sporting an unfortunate toupee which was a bit too shiny and a bit too dark. Harry inhaled the glass of wine he was sipping. The pair of them giggled. "You would just be too ashamed to go out in public like that eh?" Dionne sniggered.

"You should see what they do to us in hair and makeup" he laughed.

"Oh do tell, I love showbiz gossip," she said.

Having broken the ice, Harry and Dionne chatted through the rest of the meal, keeping the conversation light, and impersonal. She noted that he didn't ask her what she did for a living or any other personal questions.

Ralph was watching proceedings with amusement. Dionne and Lynne were his favourites, and he was pleased to see them having a good time. He had been great friends with John, and missed their lunches, his good advice, and his friendship. He also knew that John had worshipped the ground Di walked on, and would want to see her sparkling and glowing again. He was also enjoying spending a whole evening in Lynne's company. She had such a lovely way about her, her easy humour and good nature keeping her a firm favourite among London's social elite. Ralph had a crush on Lynne, which he tried to keep to himself, as he was sure she wouldn't look twice at him.

The food was exceptionally good, and Dionne discovered that Harry was extremely knowledgeable about nouveau cuisine and fine wines, which surprised her. He found himself enjoying her company, finding her easier to talk to than any woman he had ever met before.

After the meal, Ralph leaned over to interrupt Dionne and Harry, "Do you need to organise your security to pick you up?"

"They have been outside all evening, so no, they'll be ready thanks."

Harry looked quizzically. "You have security?"

Dionne squirmed a bit, "'fraid so, it can be a bit risky driving through London" hoping he would drop the subject. He looked at her as if he was trying to fathom her out.

After thanking Ralph profusely for a fabulous meal, they kissed all Ralph's protégés goodbye, and walked towards the exit. Craig immediately appeared beside Dionne, and steered them out towards the waiting Bentley. Once inside, Dionne looked out through the tinted windows to see Harry staring at the car.

Once they pulled away, Lynne started gabbling about Daniel. He had given her his number, had begged for hers, and had asked her for dinner the following Monday night. Smiling at her friend, Dionne agreed that yes, Daniel was handsome and fun, younger men were nicer, and sexier than old men, and no, the age gap wasn't huge.

Dionne had googled Harry as soon as she got home. Turned out he was 30 (according to Wikipedia), had a fairly slow rise to fame, and had been plagued by gay rumours for years, despite various girlfriends. Ok yes he was handsome, she would admit that, but too young and probably gay. She scolded herself for being a stupid, and dirty old woman.

Later that night, laying in bed, she couldn't stop thinking about the conundrum that was Harry. He really was totally perfect looking, real film star looks, but with an oddness that she just couldn't put her finger on. Something had stirred in her when he had kissed her goodbye at the end of the evening. *'Probably won't ever meet him again, so it doesn't matter,'* she thought.

Harry couldn't sleep. He had got home about 2am after going to Boujis for some drinks with the others after the meal. It had been a bit of a scrum in there, the usually blasé girls going a bit apeshit at 4 film stars in one place. One in particular had been a right pain, and had been dragged off him by the club's bouncers.

Ian had pulled a pretty little brunette and had taken her back to his place, and Josh had disappeared with twin sisters quite early, winking at Harry on his way out.

Dan and Harry got a table in the roped off VIP area, and ordered some beers.

"So you gonna see Lynne again?" Harry asked.

"Yup, taking her out to dinner Monday night. Any idea where I should take her? I need to find somewhere quiet but classy. Not the type of woman to take to the local carvery eh?"

Daniel was a touch out of his depth with fancy restaurants as he didn't really take women out to dinner first (as a rule).

"Not sure mate, maybe you should ask Ralph, he knows them, so will at least have a clue where Lynne likes to go." Harry felt quite relieved that he hadn't made the mistake of asking Dionne for a date, as he would have been churning with worry by now.

"So didn't you fancy Dionne then?" Dan dragged him back to the present.

"Out of my league mate"

"You looked like the two of you were getting on like a house on fire."

"She is a socialite. Of course she is easy to have a conversation with, would be amazed if she wasn't. Doesn't mean anything." With that, Harry tipped back his drink and said his goodbyes, before getting a cab home.

He was now laying in bed running through the evening in his mind. Annoyed that he knew nothing about her other than her dead husband, and that she had a wicked sense of humour, oh and he had a semi just looking at her cleavage. He resolved to ask Ralph about her.

The following day Lynne came round to find Dionne working in her office. Despite almost 30 years of friendship, she still didn't understand what Di did there. The banks of monitors made her eyes boggle, and the endless phone calls got on her wick. 8am was latte o clock, so Lynne picked up their lattes from Di's housekeeper, and took them into her office.

"Why the hell are you working on a Saturday morning you maniac?"

"Clearing up a few things I should have done last night, plus I have some reports to read on the Japanese junk bond situation."

"Well drink your coffee, and we can discuss this date I'm going on Monday night."

Dionne smiled at her friend. Lynne didn't work, except as unofficial shopper for Dionne. Dionne took care of all the bills because she liked having Lynne around as best pal, confidant and conscience.

"Do you know where he's taking you yet?" Dionne asked, blowing the surface of her coffee, and keeping one eye on a monitor.

"Nope. I need you to call Ralph and find out if Dan has asked, inquired or talked about me. I am depending on you Di."

"I doubt very much if either Ralph or Dan are even awake yet, so I'll pencil that job in for this afternoon. Now are you out shopping today for date clothes? I need a dress for that awards gala next week remember"

Dionne wrote a note on her desk pad -ring Ralph and spy.

"Harrods today I think," trilled Lynne. "I need an outfit, plus dresses for next week, and I ought to get waxed in case I get lucky. I've already text Louise to blowdry my hair Monday. Do you think a Brazillian or a Hollywood is best?"

Dionne pulled a face."Brazilian, Hollywood is just too pornstar."

Lynne skipped off to get ready for a day of serious shopping, and Dionne got stuck into her reports. Her mind kept wandering to a certain filmstar. Shaking her head, she tried to concentrate.

Dionne's work was her passion. When John and her had met, she had been a young girl, and they both began dabbling in some property development. A little girl in a man's world. She had started off with a small inheritance from her father which had consisted of some land in the unfashionable dockland area of London, which was now Canary Wharf. Between them they had grown a huge empire which encompassed land, commodities, bonds, shares and property. John had been the people person,Dionne the finance wizard. She missed him every day both as her business partner and her husband. They had been fortunate to have had such a good marriage, both passionate, loving people, and the perfect foil for each other.

Dionne sat and brooded about all the business meetings she had that week, which she loathed. John would have found them so easy. He had been genial and good company, able to collect friends like some people collected stamps. She had to make herself to do the schmoozing thing, and not lose people in the detail of a deal. Frowning at herself, she forced herself to focus on the report in front of her.

At around one o'clock, Connor, the butler, interrupted her with another latte and a Caesar salad. She picked up her phone and scrolled through the contacts till she found Ralph's number.

"Hiya, just wanted to say thank you for dinner last night."

"Di, hello, the pleasure was all mine I assure you. Seems like you both made quite an impression on my clients last night."

Dionne went quiet for a moment, "Daniel has asked Lynne out for dinner, did he tell you?"

Ralph chuckled, "yes, he has already phoned me for inspiration as to where to take the beautiful Lynne. If I was a cold hearted bastard, I would have said her all time favourite was the Angus steak house, guaranteed to make her horny."

"You better not, she fancies the pants off of Dan, and she's getting ratty it's been so long since she had a shag. Do me a huge favour, and point him in the direction of Nobu."

"Not the only phone call I had this morning. Harry called."

"Oh, why's that?"

"Think he was after information about the mystery lady he had dinner with last night."

A small shiver of excitement ran up Dionne's spine. "What did you tell him?"

"Just that you and I had done business together over the years."

"He didn't seem too interested in finding out anything much last night. Didn't even ask me what I did for a living, where I lived, or anything. Is he gay?" Dionne dropped that little question in at the end where she hoped it would be unobtrusive, but answered.

"Nah, don't think he bats for the other team, just seems a bit awkward around women. I thought you two got on quite well last night."

"Yeah, he was nice. Thanks. So can I count on you to send Daniel and Lynne somewhere nice for their date? Or should I warn her to wear a track suit and cancel her bikini wax?" Dionne wanted to shut down the conversation about Harry. He was inhabiting too many of her thoughts as it was. He could have got her number from Ralph if he had been interested.

"Yep, I'll make sure he picks somewhere nice. Am I allowed to tip off the paps?"

"No, you know my rules Ralph, no pictures, no publicity. That goes for Lynne too."

They said their goodbyes, and Dionne cut the call. She phoned Lynne and repeated the edited version of the conversation, omitting the bit about Harry. No point getting excited about it.

Tuesday morning at latte o clock, Lynne turned up wearing a particularly dopey grin. It turned out that Dan had taken her to Nobu for dinner, snogged her senseless on the sofa, and arranged to take her out again Wednesday night. Lynne was convinced that Wednesday night would be night-of-the-first-shag, and was practically beside herself with excitement. She sat in Dionne's office babbling happily about her date, while Dionne tried hard not to be pea green.

When Lynne had disappeared to Harvey Nicks to hunt out a new date outfit, Dionne threw herself into work. She had been buying up shares in Universal studios on the sly through various holding companies, believing them to be undervalued. She transferred all the shares from the various companies into one of her investment funds, then sat back to watch.

The shares started shooting up in value, as the markets twigged that something was happening. Her phone rang.

"What the fuck are you up to?"

"Hi Darren, how nice to hear from you. Are you keeping well?"

Darren Karrett was CEO of Wiltshire Williams, one of the biggest investment funds in the world (although significantly smaller than Dionne's).

"You know why I'm calling. Cut the chit chat, are you declaring war on Universal?"

"Now why would I do that? The shares were undervalued, any fool can see that. Or did you not look?"

"I don't do the entertainment industry, you know that. I just didn't think you did."

"I do any undervalued shares Darren, have you been watching the price go up this morning? I'm watching it shoot up as we speak. Anyway, lovely to chat, but I gotta go. Mwah."

Replacing the receiver, Dionne sat watching the screens, trying to decide whether to dump the stocks for a fast profit, or hold. She googled Harry again and found out which studio he was signed to, making the decision to hold.

Harry called Dan on Tuesday. "Got time for a beer?"

They arranged to meet up in the Punchbowl in Mayfair. Harry got there at five to one. He ordered a beer and found a table in a quiet corner to wait for Dan.

Dan arrived soon after, got a drink and sat down opposite Harry."So what's up? You didn't call me here for a catchup"

"How was your date?"

"Good thanks, why?"

Harry looked pained. Dan watched while his friend struggled to find the right words.

Finally Dan asked "Do you have a problem with me dating Lynne?"

"NO!" Exclaimed Harry,"good god, not at all. I just, erm, I, er, wanted to know, erm, a bit more, about, you know, Dionne."

"For fucks sake Harry, you are not 15, it's pretty normal to fancy someone." Dan sniggered at the thought of a movie star all in knots over a woman. Most females threw themselves at Harry.

"There's something about her. I can't figure out what she's hiding."

"Is that all that interests you about her?"

"No. She's fucking gorgeous, and I want to see her naked."

"She lives in the most fuck off house you ever saw. Lynne lives in the converted mews behind it. Gotta be fifty mill worth. That babe is loaded right up."

Harry sucked in a breath. He had figured she wasn't poor due to the bodyguards and Bentley, but right now he struggled to reconcile the funny, down to earth person who had teased a conversation out of him, with the image of a mega rich, gilded princess who lived in a palace.

"Ask her out, do you want me to get you her number from Lynne?"

Harry pondered this for a moment ,"no, but thanks". She really was out of his league. No wonder he had picked up an unattainable vibe from her.

"You sure her and Lynne aren't a couple?" Harry asked, more to be nasty than anything else.

"Definitely not mate, Lynne is definitely into men. The way she explained it is that Dionne and her have been best friends since they were kids. When Dionne was married, both her and her husband were best friends with Lynne. After Dionne's husband died, Lynne became even more important as a confidant and general make- life-better person. So Dionne earns the money and Lynne spends it"

"Like a wife" said Harry

"Yeah" agreed Dan "Don't think either of them are lesbos though."

"That'd be a sex tape worth seeing." Harry smirked.

"You really need to ask her out mate, if she is looking for a bit of male company, she ain't gonna be on the market long."

"I'll think about it."

Harry got up and went to the bar. Over more beers, they discussed their upcoming films, how uptight Universal were about budgets, and the ridiculous costume Dan had to wear for his next film.

Thursday morning Lynne didn't appear at latte o clock. She floated into Dionne's office around midday sporting a big, sloppy grin.

"You look like you swallowed a coat-hanger you dirty girl." Lynne just grinned even wider. "Good was he?"

"Oh Di, soo good. So VERY good."

"You're walking bandy."

"You are going a shade of green Di. I can soo tell you're jealous."

Dionne smiled. She was a bit jealous, but Lynne's stupid grin was infectious.

"Tell me all about your date, every detail."

Lynne settled down into the sofa behind Dionne's swivel chair. That way Dionne had to face away from the accursed monitors.

"He took me to the new Heston Blumenthal restaurant at the Mandarin Oriental. I loved it, not sure it's really his thing, but he didn't whine. We really talked. You know how you can meet someone and really connect? Well I felt we connected. Then we came back here, had coffee, and kissed for ages. Beautiful, soft, passionate kisses. Then he fucked my brains out."

Dionne spat her coffee out at that point. "You really are a romantic Lynne. Anyway, detail please."

Lynne laughed and went a bit pink." Dick size medium large, did it 3 times. Bit of a kinky bugger."

"Impressive."The two of them dissolved into giggles. "When are you seeing him again?"

"Tonight. Not arseing around with going out first though, your chef is cooking a coq au vin as we speak, for me to heat up and pretend I cooked for him. Gotta keep his strength up."

They started giggling again.

"Dionne, Harry was asking about you. Dan met him for a drink."

Dionne's tummy flipped. "What was he asking?"

"Think he was just trying to suss you out. Dan doesn't know much about you, so I don't think he could have told him much. Are you interested?"

"He is very good looking, and I'm bloody jealous of you getting shagged," said Dionne rather evasively. "I love his voice, that public school accent in his deep baritone made my knees go a bit weak." They both laughed.

"That all?" Asked Lynne, rather knowingly.

"He's clearly good looking, but I think he might be gay. I won't be making a fool of myself over him, if that's what you're asking."

CHAPTER 2

Saturday afternoon saw a team of beauty therapists set up in Dionne's dressing room under Lynne's supervision, to get the ladies ready for the awards gala that night. They both got tans, manicured, pedicured and made up. The hairdressers arrived and Dionne made the decision to wear her hair up. Louise created an intricate knot with soft tendrils left loose round her face. Lynne had her hair curled and left loose.

The dress Lynne had bought for Dionne was by Yves St Laurent. It was black, with black lace panelling, cut low at the front, and slit to the thigh. Lynne teamed it with a large diamond pendant, diamond drop earrings, and black laboutins. Looking in the mirror, Dionne stared at the sexy, slightly edgy and dangerous vixen staring back at her.

"You have truly surpassed yourself with this dress, Lynne. I love it."

Lynne was in a deep red Dior gown, her gorgeous figure shown off to best advantage.

"You are gonna pull tonight Di, I'm determined."

The Bentley pulled up outside the Dorchester. Photographers were gathered outside, lining the route in. The rest of Dionne's security detail travelled in a mercedes behind. As soon as Craig and Joe opened the car doors, the photos started. Dionne hated the flash of the cameras, it triggered her fear of publicity, but Lynne loved these functions as an excuse to dress up and look glamorous, plus they raised a lot for charity. The event tonight was a gala dinner, and awards for the business side of the film industry. They were raising money for Arpad's ARK charity, which Dionne had always donated generously to.

The ballroom was decorated beautifully, each of the damask covered tables holding a floral centrepiece, and laid with enough silverware for a lavish dinner. Vast chandeliers twinkled overhead, giving the room an opulent feel.

Lynne took two glasses of champagne from a passing waiter, and handed one to Dionne.

"We need to find the seating plan, find out which crusty old buggers we are gonna be sat next to tonight." Lynne said. She was of the belief that the dinner part was the price to pay for the dancing and mingling opportunities that happened afterwards.

"We are on the Universal table," said Dionne. Lynne's head whipped round.

"How come?"

"Kind of bought Universal." Dionne smiled non committaly. "So I'm here as the majority shareholder."

They scanned the room, sipping their drinks.

"Di!" A richly masculine baritone called out. An impossibly handsome man came striding towards them. Tall, muscular and charismatic, he wore a bespoke tuxedo in a way that made Dionne's pulse quicken. He bent down to kiss both her cheeks, while she breathed in his heady pheromones.

"I was hoping you would be here tonight. I need to talk to you."

Alessandro was an art dealer. He specialised in 20th century modern art. He was probably one of the most polished, urbane men Dionne had ever met. He was also incredibly well connected. Everything about him screamed money and breeding, from his impeccably cut hair to his perfectly tailored suit.

He tucked Dionne under his arm while he greeted Lynne. He liked Dionne as she often bought pieces from him. She trusted his judgement on the more specialised pieces, and all in all, it was a friendship he cultivated carefully.

"I have a Picasso come in, one that will excite you. I want to show it to you first before anyone else," he spoke quietly into Dionne's ear. Her eyes sparked at the prospect, she smiled up at him

"Wonderful. Your place or mine?"

Meanwhile, across the room, Harry was watching this exchange. As one of Universal's leading men, he had been invited primarily because he was in London, and would competently represent the studio. He had spotted Lynne first, then Lynne had moved aside to reveal Dionne snuggled into someone's side. He observed her smiling and chatting to the man who stood staking his claim to her. He watched Dionne leave the mystery mans arms, kiss him on the cheek, then wave him goodbye, as her and Lynne moved towards the tables.

Harry resolved to find out if it was a boyfriend. He looked like he was polished enough to be with someone like Dionne.

'God, she looks breathtaking tonight'.

He had never had such a strong reaction to a woman before. The girls who regularly threw themselves at him generally irritated him. He regarded them as vacuous air heads who were more interested in the public persona which was carefully crafted and guarded by Ralph's PR people.

Harry was interrupted from his stalking by his PR lady, who had some people she wanted to introduce to him. He stood chatting and smiling, doing the schmoozing thing as the MC's voice asked them to be seated at their tables.

Harry hadn't brought a date, he hated having to fend them off afterwards when they decided that an evening out meant that an engagement ring, or worse, would shortly follow. He knew he would be on one of the tables reserved for universal employees, so chances are he would know pretty much everyone.

By this time, Dionne and Lynne were at the table. Dionne was seated between the Vice President and the finance directors of Universal. She groaned inwardly. They were gonna be pumping her for information all through dinner.

The truth was that a tech company she owned was developing film encryption, so that movies could be filmed ready encrypted. This meant that piracy wouldn't be possible. So while the Internet had pretty much screwed the music industry, she figured the film industry would be safe, hence positioning her investments now, before it became common knowledge. Plus, the idea of being near Harry pleased her, even though she felt a bit stalkery about it.

She looked up from the menu to see Harry sitting opposite her, staring at her intently. Her stomach flipped, followed by a long forgotten tingling sensation between her legs. She smiled widely at him, watching as he went pink at being caught ogling her. He was seated too far away from her to have a conversation, but that suited him fine. He could look at her without having to worry about what he said.

The vice-president touched her arm, "we need to discuss your intentions with Universal. I need to find out if this a hostile takeover or not, and I would really like to find out if I'm losing my job or not." He looked anxious. None of them had spotted this creeping up on them, and he was convinced it was not good news.

"No need to panic. The shares were undervalued in my opinion, so represented good value, plus they diversified my portfolio nicely. There is no way I am changing the board or firing anyone. I have no interest in Hollywood except in the business sense." She crossed her fingers under the table. There was in fact a piece of Hollywood just across from her that she was indeed very interested in.

The vice-president breathed a sigh of relief. He had expected the worst. Hopefully he could get his blood pressure back under control now.

Dionne perused the table card that listed the auction lots, there were the usual signed football shirts, trips away and concert tickets. All had been donated, and would be auctioned to benefit the charity. One lot caught her eye, a dinner for two at Vertigo, the new restaurant at the top of the Natwest Tower. She quite fancied that.

Dionne leaned over to Lynne " Any auction lots you want?" Lynne picked out a handmade pair of shoes made by Manolo Blahnik, and a weekend yoga course.

After the dinner, awards were given out to various companies for technical innovation in the film industry. Universal won one for a computer generated special effect they had developed for the film Ulysses. Harry stood to accept the award on behalf of the special effects team, who were based in LA. Dionne watched him speak confidently, addressing the whole room in his melodic baritone. *'Nothing shy about him'* she thought.

After the awards, the auction began, hosted by an employee from Sothebys who also appeared on some antique program, and who seemed determined to extract the maximum money out of the well heeled gathering on behalf of the charity.

Dionne had spotted a few other high rolling financiers in the room, so was prepared to go ridiculous with her bids. The shoes went for £10500, the yoga course was £6500. Both, of course went to Dionne.

It came round the turn of the dinner for two. Vertigo was THE new restaurant of the moment. Tables were hard to get, and the chef was a famous genius bad boy.

Three of them were bidding for it, the auctioneer getting excited as the bids edged higher and higher. At £20000, one bidder fell out. It was between Dionne and Darren Karrett. She knew full well that it was now a pissing contest.

She called the next bid, "thirty grand."

Darren just looked amused and raised his hand."Forty grand."

Dionne narrowed her eyes."One hundred thousand pounds," to

gasps around her.

Darren by this time was in no mood to lose, he raised his hand, "two hundred thousand." More gasps around the room.

Laughing, Dionne shook her head. If Darren wanted to pay two hundred thousand for dinner, then fine. She would get her PA to get her a table there instead.

Harry watched all this open mouthed. She was so self possessed, so calm, and clearly so rich. He adjusted his trousers to make his current arousal a bit more comfortable, and buttoned up his jacket. *'What the fuck is happening to me?'* He thought, confused by his reaction to her. When he looked over at Dionne, she was staring at him. He pinked up, thinking that maybe she could see his erection through the table, he felt so self conscious about it.

She smiled at him, and absent mindedly stroked her index finger across her lower lip.

By the time the auction had finished, Harry was back in control of himself. As the band struck up a rendition of an old Abba song, people began to leave the tables to mingle and dance. Harry looked across at Dionne, and seeing that she was still sitting there, made a drinking motion with his hand. Dionne nodded, and Harry walked round the table to her, held out his hand to help her up, and kept hold of it until they had reached the bar, scowling as two bodyguards followed.

Harry Cooper was a man of contrasts. Classically handsome, women had been throwing themselves at him since he was a teen. He rarely enjoyed the company of ladies, and had no female friends. His mother had died when he was six, leaving five motherless boys, and a grief stricken husband. His father had never remarried, so Harry had been packed off to boarding school at the age of eight. It had been a cold, masculine place, which had caused Harry to retreat into himself.

He had been subjected to low level bullying at school, teased for being podgy and shy, things got progressively worse, until he hit puberty. He shot up to six feet tall, which sorted out his podgy issue, began working out, and joined the drama society to help with his confidence issues.

It was during this period in his life that he realised boys were attracted to him. He had a few fumbling experiences, but felt nothing, and concluded he wasn't gay. The difficulty was that he didn't seem to find women terribly attractive either.

He had tried sex for the first time when he was 18. It had been a total disaster, and a deeply humiliated Harry had realised there was a hell of a lot he didn't understand about the female anatomy, and he had no idea how to really please a woman. Female genitalia was uncharted territory to him, and he was scared of getting things wrong and hurting a woman. So Harry tended to avoid intimate relationships in general. Occasionally the studio insisted that he pretend to have a 'relationship' with an actress to give the gossip columns something to write about, and keep his 'dashing ladies man' persona alive, but he found starlets tedious and self absorbed.

His sexual tastes tended towards a specific, and in Harry's opinion, rather shameful predilection. He satisfied his cravings once a week at a club in Belgravia called 'The Chamber', which was a safe, anonymous way to indulge in his favourite pastime.

Outside of The Chamber, Harry's sex life was sporadic to the point of almost non existant, and largely unfulfilling, usually requiring a few drinks to loosen his inhibitions before he could perform.

In the company of other men, Harry was gregarious and charming. He had risen to being one of Hollywood's most popular leading men primarily because of his looks, his professionalism, and the fact that he was generally easy going and well liked. He didn't do drugs, get into fights, or generally cause PR or the studio any problems. He gazed into the eyes of his leading ladies, and could act a sex scene in one take, being careful to make his co-star feel relaxed and confident. He just couldn't do it for real.

At the age of nearly 30, Harry was used to his lack of sexual reaction, until that is, he clapped eyes on Dionne. *There's something about her, I feel something'* he thought.

They reached the quiet bar just outside the ballroom, and without letting go of Dionne's hand, Harry asked what she would like to drink.

"Champagne please."

Harry ordered a bottle of Krug, and led Dionne over to one of the tables in the bar area. The bodyguards sat at the next table, each nursing a Perrier. Dionne appeared not to notice them.

"Why were John Griffiths and Carl Mcavoy giving you a hard time earlier?" He asked.

"My company upped its shareholding in Universal this week, so they were trying to find out what I was up to, and how it would affect them. I told them they had nothing to worry about."

"What exactly do you do Dionne?" Harry asked, looking Dionne squarely in the eye.

"I'm a financier, I run investment funds, not specific to the film industry, primarily I buy land and property."

This answer both relaxed Harry, and intrigued him. He longed to see this polished, self assured woman naked and losing control at his command. The thought made his cock twitch. He shifted in his seat.

"How did you get into that?"

"I inherited some land when I was eighteen, and it went from there. My late husband and I grew the company from that."

Dionne drank in the vision of Harry's face as he sat in front of her. He was seriously gorgeous, strong jaw, wavy dark hair, clear blue eyes, and a mouth to make a sculptor weep. His muscular shoulders and narrow hips encased in a Tom Ford tuxedo made Dionne flush a bit hot. Her eyes flicked over his body. Harry noticed, *'fuck me, she's checking me out,'* he thought.

"So where do you live Harry?" Asked Dionne.

"South Ken, when I'm in London, hotels when I'm away filming," he replied, trying not to look at her chest, and failing.

"That must be horrible, living in hotel rooms for months at a time."

"Not my favourite thing, I miss my home comforts after a while."

"And what are they Harry?"

Harry paused, pondering the question. He couldn't say The Chamber, or his Xbox, or his impressive collection of Star Wars memorabilia.

"I miss English food, English telly, and having my friends nearby," he replied, pleased with his answer. "What do you do to relax?" He asked.

"I don't really, I have my office at home, so I am often guilty of working round the clock. Lynne stops me if I go more than 18 hours straight. When my late husband was alive, we occasionally watched a film, or had friends over for dinner. Since he died I don't really bother."

"That's a shame, do you like to eat out?"

"Love it, but unless its business related, I generally only go with Lynne."

"Well, seeing as you lost that bid, shall we see if my PR girl can bag a table using the Harry Cooper name?" He flashed his signature smile, "if you would join me for dinner there, that is."

The Harry Cooper signature smile was like staring directly at the surface of the sun, Dionne was transfixed.

"Love to", she smiled widely.

Harry programmed her number into his phone, and promised her he would call her as soon as a table was booked. Inside he was panicking somewhat, but drawing on all his acting skills, he concentrated on appearing calm and collected.

They wandered back into the ballroom. Dionne saw Lynne laughing with a group of friends which included Alessandro.

As the band struck up a slow song, Harry asked Dionne to dance. She wrapped one arm around his neck, as he placed his arm around her waist, holding her free hand close to his chest.

Dionne's heart was beating wildly at being in such close proximity. He smelled delicious, and felt so masculine. All she could think about was getting him naked, finding out if this reaction could carry forward into wild sex and wilder orgasms.

Harry could feel it too, it was like electricity thrummed between them. He dared not look down at her cleavage, unsure if he could control himself.

"You look beautiful tonight Dionne." Harry couldn't believe he had said that out loud.

"So do you."

"I really want to kiss you, but there are two hundred people here with camera phones, so I guess I shouldn't."

Dionne looked up, to see Harry gazing down at her, his eyes soft.

'I really want to kiss her. Fuck it, I'm gonna go for it.'

As he leaned down to kiss her, the moment was broken by the sound of gunshots and shouting. People began screaming. Smoke filled the air, causing people to panic. Harry's head jerked up, startled by the noise, he looked around for the nearest exit.

Dionne's security swooped, grabbing both Harry and her, and quickly whisking them out. Craig and Danny, the other bodyguard, held Dionne's and Harry's heads down, and got them to the door, shoving past other party goers to get their charges out. The Bentley was already outside waiting.

"In the car please Ma'am, Sir," said Craig.

"Where's Lynne?" Dionne demanded, ready to send Craig back in to get her.

Just then, Lynne was carried out in the arms of her bodyguard, figuring she would be unable to run in her high heels, he had taken no chances. He bundled her unceremoniously into the back of the car. Craig jumped in and Joe sped off. Less than two minutes ago, Dionne had been about to get her first kiss in years.

The three of them sat in shock."What the fuck just happened?" exclaimed Harry.

"Some sort of incident," said Craig from the front seat."We will find out more when we get back to the house sir."

"Probably a few Russians getting arsey with each other, they usually resolve disputes using bullets, doubt if anyone else is involved though," said Lynne. "Di, can you sort me some food at home, I didn't eat the rubber chicken, and I'm sure we're gonna be up a while waiting for news."

Dionne pulled out her phone and dialled. "What do you want to drink when we get back?" She asked Harry, "would you like me to organise something to eat?"

"Coffee would be good, and yeah I could eat if you're having something."

Lynne also asked for coffee and a snack. Harry wondered who on earth Dionne was calling at this hour, and was intrigued to see how she would magic up food.

All three of their phones began to chirp with texts, Harry's phone started ringing.

"Hi Dan, yes I'm fine, Lynne and Di are with me, their security got us out quick. What happened back there?" Dan had stayed home that evening due to an early morning ad shoot the following day, and had been watching telly.

Harry listened quietly as Dan told him what was on the breaking news on sky. He went pale as Dan told him the number of dead. Apparently people were still in there, and it was now a hostage situation. Meanwhile Dionne and Lynne were replying to texts. It seemed as though the people they knew had got out alive.

They pulled into the driveway to Dionne's house, the huge iron gates closing behind them. Harry took a sharp intake of breath as he took in Dionne's house. At one time it had been an embassy, now it was the most stunning house he had ever seen.

As they approached the front door, it swung open. A smartly dressed butler welcomed them in.

"Good evening Ma'am, refreshments have been set up for you in the drawing room," he said stiffly.

"Thanks Connor," said Dionne, handing him her handbag.

Harry took in his surroundings. They were in a huge entrance hall, with a fire burning in an enormous fireplace opposite them. The walls were a soft cream, hung with what looked like modern paintings. The overall effect was warm and inviting, but clearly expensive.

He followed them through to a large sitting room. The decor was sort of modern traditional. Expansive cream sofas, elaborate drapes, and more art, lots of art.

The enormous glass coffee table was laden with food, and carafes of coffee and hot milk. Lynne kicked off her shoes and poured them all coffee before flopping onto a sofa, tucking her legs underneath her. Dionne grabbed a remote control and pressed a couple of buttons. A large oak panel slid back to reveal a huge tv. She scrolled through the channels until she found sky news. Grabbing a bacon sandwich from the table, she sat down with the others to watch.

They saw the presenter standing outside the entrance to the Dorchester, where only twenty minutes ago they had been bundled into the car. The presenter was saying that it was believed Chechen terrorists were holding at least 50 of London's glitterati hostage inside the ballroom. Harry's skin prickled at the realisation of what a close call it had been. He had spoken to his publicist and Ralph on the way back to assure them that THE Harry Cooper was safe and well, and not trapped in some terrorist horror story.

Lynne exhaled loudly. "That was one close fucking call." She then began to peruse the food on the table, settling on a steak sandwich, and some pitta bread and hummus.

Dionne sat silently watching the news, also aware of Harry sitting in her house. She hadn't had time to think about inviting him back, or the etiquette of having a man come back to her place. All she had thought about was getting to safety quickly, and keeping him safe too.

"Your security were bloody fantastic," said Harry.

"The best money can buy," agreed Dionne.

The three of them sat in silence watching the news for another ten minutes.

"Don't they squirt in sleeping gas?"Lynne mused, "sends everyone to sleep so the SAS can go in and get the terrorists. I'm sure they did that in a situation in Russia once."

"Depends if the terrorists have booby trapped devices strapped to them or not. Did you see that film Terror in Stalingrad? That had a similar theme," replied Harry, "took a week to end the crisis in the film."

Lynne stood up and started assembling food on her plate. "If the two of you will excuse me, I'm gonna head off to bed. I need some sleep after all this excitement." Taking her plate of food, she padded out of the room, leaving her shoes on the floor.

Dionne was instantly aware that she was alone with Harry, and she needed to decide how to handle this. It was a tough one for her, with the shock of the evening, she wanted him near her, but didn't want to throw herself at him and regret it in the morning.

She looked over at Harry, he was watching the news intently, but he looked pale.

"You ok?" She asked.

Harry didn't really reply, he just nodded. Dionne moved to sit next to him, and wrapped her arms around his shoulders. He nuzzled into the crook of her neck, and pulled her onto his lap.

'She might have saved my life' he thought. *'She cares about how I feel, it's better than the chamber.'* He pushed those thoughts aside and held her tight, marvelling at how good it felt to be in her arms. He raised his head, and kissed her gently on the cheek.

"Thank you."

Dionne looked at him. "For what?"

"Not leaving me there"

Dionne smiled. That would never have happened, but she was pleased that Joe had brought them straight back here.

"Would you like me to get Joe to take you home?" She asked.

"I'm comfy here, and it's late. Don't worry I'm not propositioning you," added Harry quickly, thinking he could crash down on the sofa.

"I'm comfortable in your arms right now, but I have a guest room if you would prefer," hedged Dionne.

"Would it freak you out to let me hold you in my arms tonight Dionne?"

She disentangled from him, stood up and held her hand out. "Not at all, I need to be held."

She led Harry to her bedroom. He helped her unzip her dress before she disappeared into her bathroom. She appeared a few minutes later in a short silk pyjama set. He stared, unable to stop himself.

He shrugged off his jacket and shirt before wandering into the bathroom. He came out in just a pair of tight, jersey boxers. Dionne's mouth went dry at the sight of him. *'Perfection'* she thought.

They got into bed, Harry throwing his arm behind Di to hold her to him. Di had put the tv on and they lay silently watching the drama unfold, each grateful they weren't there.

They lay there watching as an explosion flashed across the screen. All hell broke loose as the presenter ran to a safer distance. Police and fire crews raced towards the building. People screaming could be clearly heard above the noise of the sirens and general mayhem they were witnessing. A man could be seen staggering out, supported by firemen, in a horribly burnt tuxedo, his face covered in blood.

Dionne could see the horror on Harry's face, and feel the tension in his body. She wrapped her arms tightly around him and held him tight, wondering why a big butch action hero suddenly seemed so vulnerable.

Harry held Dionne in a steely grip, worrying slightly that he would squeeze the life out of her. He could feel her heart speeding up as they watched the unfolding horror on the screen in front of them.

He stroked her arm, "we're safe, try and relax."

His touch left trails of heat down her arm, and his chest felt like a slab of solid muscle crushed against her. Feeling his soft skin pressed so close, Dionne began to feel needy and turned on. She pulled back from him slightly and ran her hand over his chest, feeling the ridges of perfectly defined pecs and abs. His breathing hitched as he realised what she wanted.

"Dionne, I know that the reason I'm here right now is because of what happened back there. I want you to know that the reason I'm holding back is not because I don't want you, I want to fuck you into next week right now, but I also want our first time to be right, and not because you need some comfort. I can hold you tonight and wait until we are both ready for more."

Dionne sucked in a deep breath. She wasn't sure if he meant that he didn't really want her, but didn't know how to let her down gracefully given they were in a compromising position, or whether to take his words at face value, and accept he was feeling as off balance as she was. Looking into his eyes, there was no hint of deception, just anxiety and longing.

"Shall I turn this tv off and see if we can get some sleep?" Dionne asked.

"Let's try."

Harry turned onto his side, taking Dionne's arm and wrapping it around his waist so she was cuddling him. Dionne listened to his breathing become slower and deeper until she finally fell asleep.

When Harry woke up, it took him a moment to remember where he was. He was alone in the huge bed, the other side cold. Looking around the room he saw a glass of orange juice on the bedside table with a note propped up against it.

Morning gorgeous

You looked like you were having a lovely sleep.

Dial 2 on the phone if you want some breakfast brought up.

I'm in my office on the ground floor.

Di xx

Harry dialled 2 on the phone on the other bedside table.

A female voice answered. "Hi Di, what can I get for you?"

Harry cleared his throat, "erm, it's not Dionne, she said to call you if I wanted anything. Any chance of some coffee?"

"Certainly sir, latte,espresso or americano? And what would you like for breakfast sir?"

This threw Harry a bit, it was like being in a hotel, not someone's house."Latte please, and an omelet if possible please"

"Certainly sir, Connor will bring it up to your room."

"Thanks."

Replacing the receiver, Harry once again wondered just how rich Dionne was. Spending the night in her arms had been a dream come true for him. No performance worries, just the incredible safe feeling of her wrapped around him. He ducked into the bathroom, locked the door and had a shower. The bathroom was larger than most people's living rooms, and was almost exclusively made of a pale, slightly sparkling marble. He perused the assorted shower gels on a built in shelf, and settled for a Jo Malone black pomegranate one, hoping it wouldn't smell too girly.

His clothes were still in there from the previous night, so after drying himself on the fluffiest towel he had ever seen, he dressed in just his trousers and shirt, rolling the cuffs up, and leaving the shirt open at the neck.

When he exited the bathroom, there was his coffee and omelet set on a small table in the bedroom. Harry sat and ate, taking in his surroundings. He was no stranger to luxury, and was wealthy in his own right by most people's standards, but this was a totally different level. He checked his phone, and replied to the dozen or so texts from people wanting to find out if he was safe.

Hooking his jacket over his arm, he ventured downstairs to find Dionne. In the foyer he ran into Lynne, on her way to see Dionne.

"Harry! You're still here! Have you seen the news this morning? 56 killed in the Dorchester last night. We were bloody lucky. The terrorists accidentally set off one of the bombs strapped to them, well that's the theory according to the bbc anyway."

"Which room is Dionne's office? She left a note saying she would be in there."

"This way."

They walked down a corridor, and Lynne stopped at the second door. She opened it without knocking. Dionne was sitting in front of a bank of screens showing market data, news, and a half written email on the screen directly in front of her.

Her office was panelled wood, rich dark colours, and an enormous antique mahogany desk, which contrasted with the technology which looked like it could have powered the space shuttle.

Dionne swung the chair round to face them. Harry bent down to kiss her cheek.

"How are you this morning? Did you manage to get some sleep?"

"Yes, although I was up early," sighed Dionne, thinking how yummy he looked with damp hair, and stubble.

"Slept like a log," piped up Lynne, "always do after champagne."

"I knew I would have a million emails this morning," said Dionne, " people checking I didn't get toasted last night."

"I had about ten texts, clearly people aren't so fussed about me," laughed Harry, making them all smile.

"Only a few million rabid fans," teased Dionne.

"So what are you two ladies planning for today?"

Dionne replied that she had a ton of work to get through. Lynne was going shopping for an outfit for her next date with Dan which she hoped would be very soon.

"Can you pick up a date outfit for Dionne while you're out please Lynne? My mission today is to book that bloody restaurant she lost the bid for." Harry smiled.

Dionne's belly clenched. She had figured he had given her the brush off last night, he hadn't been wracked with passion, so she had figured she wouldn't be seeing him again, it was all very strange.

Dionne arranged for Joe to drop Harry home.

He parted with an "I'll call you."

CHAPTER 3

"Spill" said Lynne as soon as they heard the front door close.

"Nothing to tell, we cuddled, he didn't want anything more, said it felt wrong as he was only in my bed because of events at the ball."

"How odd."

"Odd doesn't cover it really."

Lynne snorted. "Sounds like the gay rumours may have a ring of truth."

"I wouldn't be surprised," said Dionne sadly, "although I really did think he was hot for me."

"I think he's scared of you," Lynne asserted, "you are quite commanding, and the accoutrements that are around you are pretty intimidating."

"That's one theory..." Dionne trailed off.

"As you have no gossip worthy of my attention, I'm off to my yoga class."

Dionne spent the next hour googling 'Harry Cooper gay', and reading the theories his fans, and non fans had put forward. The thing that kept throwing her, was the almost-kiss in the ballroom. She had a few gay friends, and there was no way on earth they would have done that. She ran through the evening in her mind, trying to analyse the conversations. A number of theories ran through her head, including him being asexual, but no theory fitted perfectly. *'Maybe I should just wait and see how this pans out'* she thought.

Meanwhile Harry was discussing exactly the same issues with Dan.

"I cannot believe you man! You get the chance to nail a hot, single millionaire who clearly is gagging for you, and you refuse! Are you mental? Do I need to get you sectioned?"

"She's not just a millionaire Dan, bit more than that I think. I feel like the poor relation around her." Harry was commanding about ten million a film, Dan knew this. "She practically owns universal, plus a shitload of other stuff. I got some information out of her last night. Funny thing is, when you google her, nothing much comes up. Who on earth can scrub the Internet that clean?"

"And that stopped you fucking her?"

"No, what stopped me is that I want to see her again."

"You can't be that shit in bed Harry, or have you got an embarrassing dick or something?"

Harry laughed. "What the hell is an embarrassing dick? And no my dick is nice and quite large, just for the record."

"You must be shit in bed then. Don't women ever want to see you again once you've shagged them? Please don't tell me you whip 'em or stuff like that."

"Don't be daft, it's me that doesn't like going back for seconds. Drives me nuts when they think they are gonna marry me after just one shag."

"Can't see Dionne being like that."

Harry agreed. Dionne was light years away from the models and starlets he had taken to bed in the past. To change the conversation away from his lack of sexual confidence he asked Dan "so what's the deal with Lynne?"

"Not sure where it's gonna go, it's early days, you know."

"But you like her?"

"Yeah, she's alright you know, we're cool. Gonna see what happens."

"I happen to know she was outfit shopping today. Think she was hoping you would take her out again."

"Really? What did she say?"

"Not much, just that really."

"I may just give her a call. She probably needs a cuddle after last night too."

"Fuck off if you are gonna take the piss Dan." Harry laughed, "and don't you dare repeat this conversation. If I find out you have, then l will so whip your arse."

"Your secret's safe with me cuddle-bunny."

"Bastard."

Harry rang off, then immediately rang his PR company to organise that table at vertigo. He was really pleased to hear that the young PR girl at the ball had got out safely.

Dionne was reading the list of people killed in the Dorchester ballroom. She recognised a couple of names, but was thankful that none of her friends were on there. Her phone rang.

"Darren, hi, you got out ok then?"

"I did indeed, my security got me out almost as fast as yours did. So did you nail that hot film star then?" Darren always got to the point quickly.

"No, why?"

"Just nosy."

"Riiight, why would you be nosy about something like that?"

"I love a romcom, didn't you know that?"

"Darren, you are a very twisted man. So what did you really ring me for?"

"I paid 200 grand for dinner at vertigo. Would you like to join me?"

Dionne laughed, "you donated 200 grand to ARK in public, got the tax relief for it, and had all the ladies wetting their knickers at how rich and generous you are. I'm not so easy to impress Darren, take a supermodel."

"I'd rather take you." Darren's voice took on a seductive, sultry tone. Dionne felt mildly nauseous.

"I think I prefer the gobshite Darren Karrett more than this slimy Casanova persona that you're channeling."

"Ouch! You're a hard woman Dionne. We could have made beautiful music, but now we will never know. Call me if you change your mind."

"Bye Darren." Dionne cut the call with a smile. Darren Karrett might be an idiot, but he was a worthy adversary, and a bit of a kindred spirit.

Dionne set about doing some work. She bought more shares in Warner brothers, MGM, and Dreamworks rather stealthily through a network of holding companies. *'This film encryption better bloody work'* she thought.

Douggie had called her PA, Marion, and arranged lunch for later in the week, which Dionne had grimaced at, and Alessandro called to bring the Picasso round that afternoon.

He arrived around two o clock, in a sleek black Mercedes SLR, the painting in the boot wrapped in paper. Connor showed him into the drawing room where Dionne was waiting. He unwrapped the painting with a flourish.

Dionne gasped. "Wow."

Alessandro stood back and let Dionne take her time admiring the piece. He then described how it had always been in a private collection, and was only being sold due to a European aristocrat being a bit strapped for cash. It was expected to reach around ten million at auction. If Dionne didn't want it, he knew a few Russians who probably would.

"I want it," said Dionne quickly. "I can offer 9 million cash, subject to the provenance checking out."

"I will communicate that offer to my client as soon as I'm back in the office" said Alessandro smiling widely. He had known that Dionne would love it, she always loved beautiful things.

The two friends had coffee and admired the painting. They discussed the nightmare at the Dorchester, but noting that the actor fellow was clearly not around, Alessandro thought it wise not to mention him.

After Alessandro had left, Dionne went back to her office. It was a bit of a dull day on the exchanges with no big price movements. She began reading the infernally complex reports on junk bonds when her phone rang.

"Hi Harry, how's you?"

"Good thanks. You ok?"

"Yep. Bored silly with work though."

"Guess who got us a table at vertigo tonight, that is if you're free."

"Of course I'm free. The Harry Cooper name sure does open doors."

"And tables. Can I pick you up around half seven?"

"Sure. Do you want to leave your car here and get Joe to drive us, then you can have a drink?"

"Great idea. See you 7.30."

"Bye for now." Dionne cut the call and wondered if Harry would twig that she was also ensuring he wouldn't be driving home. She called Lynne.

"Lynne, he phoned. I'm going to dinner tonight. I need an outfit, hair, the works."

Lynne squealed down the phone."Leave it to me. Stop working NOW and get a shower. Don't forget to exfoliate. I'll organise everything."

"Am I being an idiot here Lynne?"

"No, you're taking a chance. You have to do it sometime, you're not meant to be lonely forever Di, John would never have wanted that for you. He would have wanted you to keep sparkling."

"Thanks."

It took precisely five minutes for Harry to start panicking at the prospect of a date with Dionne. Snuggling up to her all night had been wonderful, but he worried that having to entertain her for a whole evening would expose him as boring or unworthy. He had felt intimidated by her lifestyle and awed by her home. The only thing that stopped him from cancelling was his extreme physical attraction to her, which had been a bit of a first for him. *'Its no good, I have to see her naked, I have to try,'* he thought, trying to quell his nerves.

Dionne took Lynne's advice and wrapped up her work for the day, but not before speaking to her security adviser about Harry. She requested full searches on him. Adam Fairchild was an expert who would be guaranteed to find anything there was to find.

She took her time in the shower, applying a hair mask, and following Lynne's instructions regarding exfoliation. When she was finished, she sat and carefully applied body lotion that matched her perfume, and dabbed just a touch of scent to her wrists and behind her ears.

Lynne arrived back, accompanied by Louise, Dionne's hairdresser, and Susie, the makeup artist.

"I'm thinking evening, but natural, not too heavy a look." Lynne instructed Susie. "Oh and she's wearing maroon, but keep the lips sheer. Dark looks vile on her."

"Lynne, I'm nervous. I can't believe I'm nervous, but I am. Suppose we have nothing to say, or he turns out gay, or, or."

"Will you shut up. You are 40, not 14, and you are Dionne Devere, not some chavvy kid with no idea how to carry a conversation. If it turns out he bats for the other team, then you get a nice meal out, and a new friend. If he's straight, you might even get laid. So will you quit whining, and let me concentrate. I'm thinking the maroon Roland Mouret dress, kitten heel matching shoes so you don't fall over, and darker maroon jacket. I think easy on the jewellery tonight, we won't whack him in the face with your diamond collection just yet. All sound ok?"

"Yes mien fuehrer, fine, you know best."

"I do indeed, now have you got condoms?"

Dionne blushed. "No,why would I have condoms?"

"You don't know where he's been. I picked you up a box, and some other things you might need, and put them in your bedside cabinet."

"You think of everything. Dunno what I'd do without you."

"You'll never find out. Now hair."

Dionne tuned out Lynne and Louise's discussions regarding her hair, silently musing on the prospect of the first sex since John.

'How will I pluck up the courage? Will it be awkward? What will he

expect?' With all these thoughts running through her head, she sat quietly while Louise began blow drying her hair.

Harry arrived at precisely 7.25. He was buzzed through the gates by Joe, and neatly parked his Aston Martin next to the Bentley. Connor opened the front door as he approached.

"Good evening sir, Mrs Devere is expecting you. Please take a seat and I will let her know you have arrived."

Harry sat on one of the sofas in the foyer and waited. Two minutes later, Dionne and Lynne came down the stairs.

Harry stood, "You look stunning," he said, eyeing her appreciatively.

"Thank you, you look pretty good yourself," said Dionne, "shall we head off?"

"Have a great time," said Lynne," see you tomorrow," and with that Lynne made her way down the corridor and through to her own house.

They got into the Bentley, Harry was surprised that Craig got in the passenger seat. "Your security coming too? Should I have booked him a table?"

"Security comes everywhere, but don't panic, he'll just sit in the bar with a Perrier."

Inhibited by the presence of others in the car, they both sat quietly through the journey listening to an Adele CD that Joe had put on.

There were no photographers outside the restaurant, which surprised Dionne. She had expected either Harry's PR, or the restaurant itself to tip off the paps that the famous Harry Cooper was dining there tonight.

"I said no publicity" said Harry, reading her mind."I didn't want you splashed all over the gossip blogs tomorrow morning, I know you hate that type of thing."

'Hmm, clearly he's been listening to Ralph' thought Dionne."Yes you're right, thanks for that."

The journey up in the lift was an exercise in surviving sexual tension. The three of them stood awkwardly in the small space as they travelled up to the 42nd floor.

The restaurant was gorgeous, all dark wood, jewel coloured accents and classic white starched tablecloths. They were seated three tables back from the bar, in a decently private spot, with an exceptional view, being directly next to one of the giant windows.

The menus were fairly short, and once they had chosen, Harry ordered for both of them, he also chose a red wine to go well with their steak. Dionne began to think that maybe she had underestimated Harry, tonight he seemed so urbane and in control. She had been guilty of imagining him to be younger and less capable than he actually is.

'I'll have to watch myself with that' she thought.

They chatted about Harry's next film, which was to begin shooting in about two months in LA, the pre-production and costume fittings involved, and his co-stars, including some gossip about the female lead involving a wig, a joint, and the cops that made Dionne giggle.

"Are film sets very druggie places then?" Dionne asked.

"It's always available. Not my thing though, is it yours?"

"No. I think Lynne has indulged a few times, but it's not my scene."

"I thought share dealers and the like took coke to concentrate and stay awake," probed Harry.

"I'm not a share dealer per se, and I've never worked in the city, I've always worked in my own company. I'm more of an espresso abuser," said Dionne, unsure of this conversation.

"I know you pretty much own universal, but what exactly do you do for a living Di, you're pretty enigmatic about it." Harry wasn't letting go.

"I invest in stuff, mainly land, buildings, some companies, that kind of thing, but you know that already."

"On who's behalf?"

"Mine."

Harry looked at her intently. "So it's your own money you play with, not other investors?"

"Correct, now is it my turn to ask probing questions Harry?" Dionne tried to add a playful note.

"Fire away."

"Are you gay?"

Harry stared incredulously. "No I'm most certainly not! Do you think I would be asking you for dinner if I wasn't interested?"

Dionne visibly relaxed, her big question answered. *'He's interested'.*

"Have you been reading shit on the Internet? There are gossip sites for old queens that would have you believe every man in Hollywood is gay."

"Yeah, I read them," admitted Dionne," I did wonder why Hollywood never employed any straight men though, after reading that every actor I ever heard of was a raging closet case." They both laughed.

"Tell me about your late husband, how did you meet?"

"We met at school. As friends at first, then we began dating when I was 16, John was a few years older than me, so had left school and was working for a property developer. We got married when I was 20. We were married for 18 years. He died about two years ago."

"Can I ask how he died, or is that too painful for you to talk about?"

"No it's fine. He died of a heart attack while in his doctor's office. He had heart problems for a few years and was having some routine tests done. He was walking on the treadmill when he had a sudden, catastrophic cardiac arrest. Dead before he hit the floor, that's what his doctor said. Good way to go really, if you had a choice that is."

"Hard for you though." Harry said softly.

"The suddenness was the hardest thing. One minute he was walking out the door saying see you later, the next he had gone. That, and the fact that he was so young. I felt cheated for him."

"I can understand that. My mother died when she was only 34, giving birth to my youngest brother. As a kid, it felt unfair on me, as an adult I feel it was unfair on her." Harry admitted.

"Must have been very difficult for you, losing your mum at that age?"

"Yes it was, although it was a long time ago now."

"So, changing the subject, what made you decide to become an actor Harry? Money, women or fame?" Dionne asked in a teasing voice.

"Money really," admitted Harry, "a talent scout was a parent at my school, and saw me in the school play. He said I had the right look for a film he was casting and it went from there. I left school and began my first film, much to my Father's disgust." Harry pulled a face as he recalled unpleasant memories." Did some tv work, did some supporting roles, then started getting the leading roles. I'm a bit typecast really, as in I generally play action heroes. It's a bit of a pain because it means keeping my body looking a certain way, but it pays well, and they are fun to do. I'm a bit shit at the romantic hero thing."

"Oh I don't know, I could see you in an erotic sex scene," flirted Dionne.

"I'm quite inhibited when it comes to sex," admitted Harry."Boys school and all that."

"You must have women throwing themselves at you every day, I can't believe you wouldn't enjoy the trappings of fame."

"All they want is to shag the film star, they don't ever want to see the real me. Plus I had some bad experiences with groupies that scarred me a bit."

Dionne raised her eyebrows and stayed silent, prompting him to go on.

"By the time I lost my virginity, I was already working on my first film. I had no idea what I was doing and she humiliated me. I then had a couple of women who figured that because I'm muscular and strong, I would want it rough and painful. Bloody hurt me. Now I flinch when anyone touches my dick." He blushed. "That was too much information wasn't it?"

Dionne looked at him with compassionate eyes. "Not at all, it explains a lot, and it answers a lot of my fears, so no, it's never too much information when I'm trying to understand, and get to know you."

"You have fears? What sort of fears do you have? I can't imagine you being scared of anything, you seem so, well, confident." Harry was shocked at her confession. She seemed so polished to him.

Dionne took a deep breath. She knew she had to share her fears as openly as he had shared his. She began hesitantly, "I am horribly aware that I'm ten years older than you, that the girls you have been with were most likely models, and that for the last 20 years, I've only had sex with one man. To start again from scratch is terrifying. I'm even scared of undressing in front of you. How sad is that?" She sat quietly as he just stared at her, his mind reeling at her revelation.

"First of all Dionne, your age makes you more attractive, not less, as does the fact that you had a happy marriage with John. It shows me that you know how to love someone. Secondly, my experiences with those models were largely unpleasant, and in some cases scarring as I said before. Beauty on the outside doesn't mean beauty on the inside. Anyway, you are stunningly gorgeous. Just because you aren't six foot tall doesn't make you unattractive. I like the fact that you are dinky. I personally can't wait to see you naked. I've been thinking about nothing else since we met."

Everything south of Dionne's waist tightened viciously. She shifted in her seat. "Well I can promise you one thing Harry, I will always be gentle with you."

"Thank you. I can promise you the same."

They spent the rest of the meal chatting about the places they had travelled to, and enjoying the superlative food and wine. The two of them admired the amazing views across London at night, picking out landmarks. Harry gazed at the vista, feeling as though he was experiencing the best night of his life.

Harry paid the bill, and they left holding hands. He stole a glance at her in the elevator, his anticipation building with every passing minute. They slid into the waiting car, and, again, inhibited by the security crew, spent the journey back in silence, each lost in private thought.

CHAPTER 4

Back at the house, they had coffee in the drawing room. Dionne had plugged her iPod into a concealed dock, and the room was filled with the strains of Will Young. They sat on the large sofa, each slightly turned so that they were almost facing each other. Harry trailed a finger down her face, stroking softly down her neck,

"So soft, so beautiful," he breathed. He leaned in and kissed her softly, almost chastely. Her arms lifted to touch his shoulders, to run her fingers through his hair, she marvelled at how thick and soft it was.

He deepened the kiss, stroking his tongue over her lower lip until hers shyly came to meet him. Their tongues engaged in an erotic dance, tasting and inflaming the other. His hands explored her neck, her shoulders and her back. She felt so soft and compliant in his arms, *'so right'* Harry thought. He couldn't remember ever being so turned on by a woman.

Dionne pulled away from his kiss, and they stared into each others eyes. Abruptly she stood, and not saying a word, held out her hand. He took it, and she led him upstairs.

They stood in the bedroom facing each other. Harry wrapped his arms around her and kissed her more deeply this time, caressing her back. She reached up and slipped his jacket off his shoulders, turning slightly to throw it over a nearby chair. She unknotted his tie, letting it drop to the floor, then unbuttoned his shirt. Stroking his chest, she groaned into his mouth, he felt so perfect, so muscular. He reached around and unzipped her dress, letting it slide down her body into a pool on the floor.

He stepped back to look at her."Such perfection," he breathed, his strong hands roaming over her bottom. He kicked off his shoes and socks, and held his breath when she undid his trousers and pushed them over his hips.

He ran his hands over her breasts until he could feel her nipples lengthen under the lacy fabric. Dionne reached behind her and undid the bra to allow Harry to slide it off her. He bent down to take a nipple in his mouth, and laved his tongue over it, causing waves of sensation to run through Dionne's core.

They stumbled towards the bed. Harry slid his Calvin Kleines over his hips, then pulled Dionne's lacy knickers down. They fell onto the bed, their bodies tangling, all thoughts of shyness forgotten.

"I want to make you come Di, tell me how to make you come," whispered Harry, tracing a finger round one of her breasts. *I need to get this right for her'* he thought.

"Lick me, softly, gently" begged Dionne. She guided Harry to slip two fingers inside her and curl them upwards to find her spot, and shaking, showed him where his tongue would drive her wild. She was so turned on that she wouldn't let him stay there for long, she wanted him inside her when she came.

Harry watched her writhing with pleasure, marvelling at how easy it had been for her to teach him what she liked. He was glad when she stopped him, he wanted to fuck her so much that he was worried how long he would last if he carried on tasting her. He knelt between her legs.

"Condoms, top drawer." Dionne muttered, unable to take her eyes off his huge, throbbing cock. He found them and unrolled one over himself.

Almost mindless with need, Dionne positioned the head of his cock at her entrance and guided it in. Resting over her on his elbows, Harry began to move, feeling as though his whole body was currently centred in his cock. He moved slowly at first, trying to make it last, so turned on, he knew if he moved any faster it would all be over.

Dionne reached between them to massage her clit, loving the feeling of fullness, and the sensation and sight of this beautiful man moving above her.

Harry was aware of her legs stiffening, and felt her rippling around his cock, then suddenly she came. She cried out his name as she pulsed around him, tipping him over the edge, giving him the most intense orgasm he ever had.

'I made her come! I can't believe it, I actually made her come!' He thought, delighted with himself.

They stayed in that position until their breathing and heartbeats slowed. He drew out of her and laid beside her.

"Wow," said Dionne.

"Yeah, that was astounding," agreed Harry. "I've never had sex like that before."

Dionne turned to face him, tracing her finger gently over the ridges of his abs. "Really?"

"Yeah, really. I've never been so turned on in my life."

She grinned up at him. "You really are gorgeous in every way. Lets do that again in a bit."

He beamed at her "I loved it when you came. Made me feel like a god."

"We got over the naked issue pretty easily," Dionne teased.

Harry propped himself up on one elbow and raked his eyes over her body. "You have nothing to be shy about Dionne, you are a goddess in every way, you look amazing, feel amazing and taste amazing. I can honestly say you have the best tits I've ever seen."

Dionne giggled. "I did notice you looking at them at the ball."

"I did try not to, but it's difficult when they look so delicious."

"Am I going to be allowed to taste you?" Dionne enquired, seeing him starting to get aroused again. *'Again? So quickly? Wow'* she thought.

"Erm, it makes me a bit nervous, but I'm happy to let you try. Erm, no teeth though. Is that ok?" Harry said. His reply made Dionne wonder what on earth his experience with THAT had been.

She began by kissing the tip, then softly licking the head before tracing the veins down his shaft with her tongue. He became stone hard immediately. She kissed his inner thighs with featherlight kisses, then licked over his balls, alternating with soft kisses. His garbled pronunciation of her name confirmed that she was pleasing him. Licking up and down his shaft, she reached up to caress his nipples, rolling them gently between her fingers.

"Oh god, Dionne, that feels so good."

"Tell me what you like, what will please you."

"Lick my balls again please." Harry's voice was husky, thinking that this was the most erotic encounter he had ever had. Dionne teased him, alternating kisses with soft, lush licks, until his cock started throbbing and leaking pre-cum.

Harry reached over to the bedside cabinet and grabbed another condom. Once on, he pulled Dionne back up to straddle him. She lowered herself onto his erection, leaning forward to give him a searching kiss. With him stretching her, she worked herself to a frenzy sliding up and down his thick cock. By this time she was mindless with the need to orgasm, so she massaged her clit with her fingers while Harry gazed up at her in awe.

"Oh my god, you feel so good." Dionne panted, as her body quickened.

Harry took her nipples in his fingers and rolled them gently. This pushed Dionne over the edge, and she came around him, pulsing and shaking.

Watching her lose control riding his cock caused Harry to have such a strong orgasm himself that it almost hurt. When they had cleaned up, Harry pulled Dionne into his arms, and held her until they both fell asleep.

Harry woke up first, turning his head to see Dionne sleeping next to him, he smiled at the memories of the night before, and the little panda smudges round her eyes where she had been too busy to think about taking her make up off. He ever so gently cupped her breast, which woke her up. She stretched, arching her back, pushing into his hand, and opened her eyes. Seeing him gazing at her, she smiled lazily.

"Morning beautiful."

"Morning beautiful yourself."

She shifted onto her side, facing him, and stroked his face. Her hand moved to stroke his shoulders, then his ribs. His skin felt like silk. Harry felt himself stirring, he ran his hands over her hips and backside, then back to her breasts.

When Dionne's hands lowered to touch his erection, Harry flinched. "Sorry," he said, "force of habit."

Dionne immediately moved her hands to stroke his back, not acknowledging his flinch, just revelling in the warm, sexy man laying next to her. For the next hour they made love slowly and languidly.

Afterwards, they lay there a while to calm their breathing. Harry reflected on what he was by now considering his sexual awakening.

His reverie was broken when Dionne asked "would you like some coffee, or would you prefer tea?"

"Coffee please."

Harry didn't want to break the spell of their fabulous time

together. He turned to Dionne, "no regrets?"

"None at all. Amazing sex with a Greek god? How could anyone knock that?" Dionne laughed.

"So have you any plans for today? Do you work on a Sunday?" Harry asked.

"I often do, but there's nothing that can't keep. So what have you got in mind?"

Harry hadn't actually made any plans, and was grasping for ideas for the day. All he knew was that he wanted to be with her.

"I didn't make any plans for today either, so maybe I could take you out to lunch somewhere? Or are there any movies you want to see?"

Dionne was so unused to having free time that she was a bit stumped as to what they could do. Apart from work, her life was pretty empty, and she relied on Lynne to fill it. She felt quite comfortable with Harry, and a little bit of her didn't want him to go. Another little bit of her felt uncomfortable that she didn't want him to go home.

"Do you need to go home for a change of clothes?" She asked.

Harry flushed a bit (which Dionne thought was adorable) and said "My dry cleaning is still in the boot of my car, and my gym bag, so I have clean clothes, I just have to get them out."

"Connor will do that for you," said Dionne, as she dialled down to the housekeeper for their coffees.

Dionne slipped on a robe before the butler arrived with their drinks. She gave him Harry's car keys, and shortly afterwards, Connor arrived with an armful of plastic covered clothes and a holdall. Harry sat up in bed and watched as Connor disappeared through a doorway to the right, and appeared a few minutes later empty handed except for his car key.

"There's another bathroom and some clothes rails in there," explained Dionne.

She watched as Harry wandered naked over to the door, his movements lithe and graceful, musing that it was almost as if Adonis himself had come to visit.

Harry took in the bathroom. It was a masculine space, primarily made of black marble. Unlike the other ensuite which he had seen on his first visit, this had no bath, just a giant hi tech shower. He found his wash bag inside his holdall, and had a shave. It took him a while to work out the buttons for the complex array of jets and spray heads , so once he figured it out, he ended up just having a quick shower. Connor had hung up his dry cleaning in the adjoining dressing room, which had metres of empty clothes rails. Harry nosed round for a bit, finding out that all the drawers in the dressing room were empty. In the vanity unit of the bathroom, all he found was a new toothbrush in its packet, toothpaste, and some shower gels.

Meanwhile, Dionne stared at the panda smudges, and rumpled hair in her bathroom mirror.

'I can't believe he fancied me looking like this.'

She grabbed her cleanser and cleaned off the remnants before jumping in the shower, hoping the hot water would ease the muscles currently aching from all the hot sex.

'Jesus, I'm out of practice. Hope he doesn't expect this every night.'

After drying herself, Dionne wandered into her dressing room and pulled on a pair of black jeans, and a cashmere t shirt, and went to find Harry.

"Did you work out that infernally complicated shower?" Asked Dionne when Harry wandered back into the bedroom.

"Yep, took me a while to figure it out though," he laughed. He was wearing casual chinos and a plain t-shirt, which clung to the muscles of his chest and arms. Dionne found herself staring.

She took his hand, "come get some breakfast," she said, leading him out of the bedroom before she jumped him again.

She took him downstairs into her breakfast room, where Connor had laid out some dishes on hot plates. Harry chose full English, Dionne poured them both orange juice and coffee before popping eggs benedict on a plate for herself.

During breakfast, Harry asked about her family and background. Dionne explained she was an only child and her parents had been middle class. Harry told her about growing up with four brothers. His father had been fairly well off, but hopeless at any sort of domestic task, so after their mother died, the boys were all packed off to boarding schools as soon as they reached eight, and went feral in the holidays.

When they finished their meal, Harry asked if he could have a tour of the house. They started in what Dionne referred to as the East Wing. She showed him her office, which led through to her PA's office, and a filing room. Harry whistled through his teeth as he took in the banks of monitors. Next up was a large, ornate, dining room for formal dinners with a huge table to seat 20 people.

"I don't use this room very often," admitted Dionne.

The last room they came to on that side of the house was a library. All dark wood and oxblood leather chairs. The walls were lined with books from floor to ceiling. A large fireplace dominated the room, with squashy leather chairs in front. Harry walked into the room and scanned some of the book titles, finding that there seemed to be a lot of contemporary fiction.

"Are you into reading then?" He asked.

"Yes I am, but my taste is more Ruth Rendall than Thomas Hardy," admitted Dionne, a bit embarrassed.

'I never claimed to be an intellectual, and he's only a bloody actor,

who am I trying to impress' she thought.

She stood in the doorway, trying to move him out of the library before he discovered her Jackie Collins collection.

They moved on to the West Wing. Harry had already seen the drawing room, so they skipped that. Next was the breakfast room where they had eaten, so they skipped that too.

A corridor led through to the kitchen, which was vast, and had a similar feel to a commercial kitchen. Dionne explained that on the other side of the kitchens were staff accommodation, and the offices for her security team.

"Do your staff work 24 hours?" Asked Harry.

"Yes, sometimes I work through the night, and anyway the security teams are on duty 24 hours, so they need feeding."

'Bloody hell, this is so out of my damn league' thought Harry.

They walked back to the main corridor, and Dionne opened the next door to reveal a sumptuous games room. It held a giant plasma tv at one end, below which were games consoles. A large sectional sofa arrangement was directly facing the tv. Another wall was dedicated to a bar, with optics artfully arranged. It was large enough to rival a commercial bar, and looked like it was the work of an extremely talented designer. At the far end of the room was a billiard table, with a lamp over it. Harry's eyes widened.

"This is really wow," he stuttered.

Dionne was quiet. The room had been mainly Johns, but seeing Harry's reaction, she didn't feel inclined to tell him. *'I will not keep going on about John,'* she thought.

Harry wandered round the room, taking in the art on the walls. He checked out the games next to the consoles, and took in the antique carved billiard table.

"This place is unbelievable Di," said Harry, feeling intimidated.

"Thanks," she replied. "You haven't seen my piece de resistance yet."

She led Harry out of the games room to the final doorway. She opened it, and gestured to him to go in. He walked in to a vast orangery, built around what looked like an olympic sized pool. Around the edges were cream tiles, with artfully placed Grecian urns, arrangements of ferns, and Greek statues. There was a delicate wrought iron bistro table and chairs placed beside another bar. Lynne was doing lengths of the pool. She stopped when they came in, and trod water.

"Hi Harry, how was your dinner last night?" Lynne asked, looking slyly at Dionne.

"Fabulous! Loved it," replied Harry.

"Just giving Harry a tour of the house," said Di, hoping Lynne would keep quiet.

"I'll be out in a bit, few more lengths to do," said Lynne before resuming a surprisingly fast front crawl.

"Lynne's house is through that doorway there," said Dionne, pointing to a door directly ahead at the far end of the pool.

"I did wonder how she got home barefoot the other night," admitted Harry.

Dionne showed Harry the gym adjacent to the pool, then showed him around upstairs, noticing that he was getting quieter and quieter as the morning went on.

Outside Dionne's bedroom, Harry pulled her round into a kiss. She deepened it, stroking his tongue with hers, wrapping her arms around his neck.

"You ok?" She asked, "you seem very quiet."

"Yeah I'm fine," he replied, a troubled look on his face. "It's just...nothing, it's fine."

"C'mon, share, something's clearly bothering you," pressed Dionne.

Harry exhaled loudly. His mind was racing as he struggled to find the words to convey how he felt. "The thing is, um, I've never met anyone I've reacted to like I react to you, and then it turns out that you are so far out of my league it's untrue, and I'm worrying that I'm reading too much into everything and over thinking things. I just feel that you could have any man on the planet, and would get bored with me real quick."

"What? Are you nuts? First off Harry, you are gorgeous, second, you're great company, third, how many men would put up with a workaholic with no idea how to use a morning off apart from getting you naked again?"

They both smiled tentatively at each other before Harry grabbed Dionne, and carried her back into the bedroom. He pulled her t-shirt over her head and kissed down her neck to the swell of her breasts at the edge of her bra, running his hands over her ribs and her waist. Kneeling in front of her, her undid her jeans, and slid them down her legs. Dionne reached round and undid her bra, throwing it on the floor. She stepped out of her shoes and jeans, and watched as Harry hooked his fingers into the band of her knickers and slid them down her thighs.

"Ok, so you got me naked, what are you going to do to me?" Breathed Dionne.

"I want to make you scream my name. Tell me how to do that."

Harry threw his clothes off quickly and tugged Dionne onto the bed. He planted featherlight kisses up the inside of her leg until he got to the apex, then stopped and kissed up the inside of her other leg.

Dionne's hips started to sway. This was slower and more deliberate than their earlier lovemaking. The anticipation of seeing and feeling this beautiful man and his beautiful thick cock making love to her again, caused a surge of arousal through her, and she could feel herself getting slick and hot.

Harry began to lick her, deep lush licks, that made her body arch off the bed. He carried on almost French kissing her intimately, before slipping a finger inside her to slowly stroke her g spot.

Dionne could feel herself building, but wanting more for him, she said in a low voice, "look in the second drawer down, there is a small vibrator. If you fuck me hard with that pressed onto my clit, you will hear me scream."

He fumbled round in the drawer, found it, plus a condom. After slipping the condom on, he knelt between her legs and staying upright, entered her. Dionne heard the click then buzz of the vibrator, and braced herself for the onslaught. As soon as it touched her, the combination with his cock sliding in and out took her soaring higher and higher. Harry watched Dionne, enraptured, marvelling at how he could elicit so much reaction from her, his own anticipation building to levels he had no idea even existed.

Dionne came with a scream, her body practically exploding into a fierce orgasm that wrung her inside out. Her sudden clenching inside, the sight of her in ecstasy, and the sound of her calling his name, tipped Harry into his own release, with an intensity that shocked him. He collapsed onto her, remaining inside her, feeling her pulsating around his cock.

After what felt like hours, but was in reality just a few minutes, he pulled out of her, and laid down beside her.

"Is it always like this?" He asked.

"It's pretty special with you," answered Dionne, a bit evasively.

'Hmm, he really is inexperienced. That's unexpected' she thought.

"I can't seem to get enough of you, I don't know what it is, but I could be inside you forever and it wouldn't be long enough."

Dionne's heart hammered inside her chest. This was all too fast, she knew she had to pull him back at some point. The trouble was, she was falling too. She gazed at his beautiful face, watching as the emotion flashed in his eyes.

"So, now you know how to make me scream, we have to figure out how to do the same for you. I need to take you on your sexual adventure," she purred.

"That sounds a bit, um, scary. When you screamed as you came, did I hurt you?" He enquired.

"No, not at all, it was just a very intense orgasm. It sort of pushes a scream out of me when I come like that. It wasn't painful in any way."

"What's a sexual adventure?" Harry asked, worry wrinkling his brows.

"It means trying things out together, with the focus on finding out which sensations give you the most pleasure. We try stuff, and see what you like. It could be something as simple as a fur glove rubbing your dick, right through to, well, whatever it is that flips that switch."

'Bloody hope it doesn't turn out something pervy' thought Dionne.

"That sounds amazing. Are you on the pill?" Harry asked, breaking her reverie.

"No, I can't have kids, so I never had to bother. Maybe you should get tested for STD's, then we won't need to bother with those damn condoms."

"I got tested after my last encounter, so I know I'm ok, and if you haven't been active for a few years, you are probably fine too," said Harry, getting aroused again.

"I'm very intrigued by your lack of sex life. Do you have a kink? Most men are horny all the time, so if you avoided women as much as you claim, what did you do?" Probed Dionne.

"Well, I like porn, I work hard, workout everyday, and had kind of accepted my lot in life, until I met you, that is. What you have to remember is that I spent a lot of time away shooting, so relationships would have been difficult. Groupies and one night stands have always scared me, so it was easier to avoid them. The bloody gay rumours do drive me nuts though," he laughed.

"I think we established that there is NOTHING gay about you," said Dionne, bending down to run her tongue along his erection.

For another hour, they lost themselves in each other.

"Can I take you out for lunch, I know a great little bistro in Chelsea?" asked Harry when they came up for air.

"Ok, I'll just let security know," replied Dionne. "How come you don't have security? I would have expected the studio to have provided you with a bodyguard."

"Male leads don't tend to be perceived to be at risk. Apart from the odd crazy fan, I get left alone pretty much. Why do you have 24 hour bodyguards?"

"What I've built really. People like to have a pop at the rich. Plus, if anything were to happen to me, there would be economic repercussion. That's why I try and stay anonymous as far as I can. I couldn't bear the thought of appearing on the Forbes list, and the whole world knowing what I do, and wanting to punish me because of it."

Harry was thoughtful. "So is me being famous gonna be an issue?" he asked.

"Possibly. I figure that as long as we keep things low key, and I don't hang off your arm at premieres, it should be fine, but I would feel happier if you had a security team."

Harry drove them over to Chelsea, with just Craig in the back of the car. Dionne watched him drive, enjoying seeing him handle the powerful car so confidently. The bistro was delightful. Small, intimate and family run, the food was authentic, and the wine list superb. Dionne took the opportunity to do some people watching. They guessed at the occupations of the other patrons, and giggled at an eccentric looking gentleman who arrived with two poodles.

A lone woman walked into the bistro, and sat at the next table. She was one of those nondescript people, dressed in brown, with mousy hair cut into a sensible bob. Harry noticed that she was staring at him over her menu.

"Excuse me, but are you Harry Cooper the actor?" She asked.

"Erm yes" replied Harry.

"I love all your films, you're my favourite actor. Would you mind if I had an autograph?"

Harry took a pen from her, and signed a scrap of paper she thrust at him, noticing that she was giving Dionne a hostile look.

"Thank you. I loved you in 'War of the gods' saw that film about twenty times. Is this your mother?" She gestured at Dionne, who was horrified.

"No it isn't," snapped Harry, "and if you don't mind, I'm having a quiet lunch."

"Oh I see," said the woman, her face contorting in annoyance, "us fans are good enough when you want us to see your films, but not when it suits you. There's no need to be so stuck up, it was only a sodding autograph."

At that point, Craig came over. "Everything all right here?" He asked, eyeing the strange woman warily. The woman stomped back to her own table, grabbed her bags and walked out. Harry breathed a sigh of relief.

"All fine now thanks Craig, although I'm not happy about being mistaken for your mother," said Dionne." This is exactly why you need security Harry."

"She's just a fan, it's no biggie," dismissed Harry, "and you most certainly don't look anywhere near old enough to be my mother Di, she just said that to be nasty."

Hollie Cranwell sat on a bench round the corner from the bistro and sobbed. All those years of loving Harry Cooper, and her one meeting with him, he was so horrible. She had followed his career for years, ran the Harry Cooper fan page on Facebook, and had carefully kept all his newspaper articles in special scrapbooks.

'How dare he' she thought. *'Humiliating me like that, and who was that bitch?'* In her fantasy world, Harry was celibate because he was waiting to meet her.

'I'll get him, how dare he dismiss me for her. How dare he cheat on me.'

CHAPTER 5

Heading back to the house, Dionne's phone rang.

"Alessandro, how are you?" Dionne answered. Harry lips flattened into a grumpy line.

"No I've not been in my office this morning to check emails. Oh that's fantastic news. Have you heard back from my lawyer yet regarding provenance? Brilliant. I'll drop the money into your account later. Can you bring it over tomorrow? Super, thanks Alessandro, ciao sweetie"

"What did he want?" Harry asked, a hint of annoyance in his voice.

"I bought a painting off him last week. Apparently my offer was accepted and my lawyers happy it's all kosher."

"Oh ok. I think he fancies you, I was watching him at the Dorchester drooling over you," said Harry, feeling jealous.

Dionne laughed. "I think he's more likely to fancy you than me poppet, and I fear that even you are far too old for his tastes."

"Really? Oh my god, I got that one wrong then. I never had a good gaydar." They both started laughing.

Harry sat on the couch in Dionne's office as she checked her emails, and replied to a few. He watched, mesmerised, as her fingers flew over the keyboard, and wondered who was bothering her on a Sunday.

Lynne walked into the study, and flopped down onto the couch next to Harry. "Where did you two disappear to? I came looking for you when

I finished my swim," she huffed.

"Harry took me to lunch in a great little bistro in Chelsea. You would have loved it," said Dionne, not looking up from her screen. She had spotted an email from Adam Fairchild, but decided not to open it until she was alone. *'Don't want to look like a stalker '* she thought.

"Oh well thanks for inviting me. Not. Anyway, Dan called while you were out. He's coming over this evening. Shall we make it four for dinner? We could all bond over super mario in your games room."

"What a great idea, Dan's a real laugh. Are you up for it Di?" Harry asked.

'That means he wants to stay another night, hmm, not sure about that, I need some sleep.'

"Yeah, good, but I do need an early night though." Dionne noticed Harry tense as soon as she said it.

"Good, cos I already spoke to chef, and he's doing a roast. I found out its Dan's favourite dinner." Lynne said as she picked up the phone to dial the kitchen for some coffees for them all.

Harry was watching Dionne intently, her comment had put him instantly on edge.

'Am I being a one night stand she can't get rid of? Am I overstaying my welcome?'

"I can go home tonight if you're tired Di."

Dionne didn't answer, she felt torn between wanting him with her, and worry that this was becoming too intense too fast. She did, however hear the little catch of anxiety in his voice, which surprised her. It also surprised her how much she cared that he was unsure of her.

"A roast and super mario sounds good, and shall we see how we feel later?" Dionne chose her words carefully, not taking her eyes off her screen. She certainly didn't want to look directly at Harry in case his eyes betrayed his hurt.

Lynne picked up Dionne's mood, and figured that her friend was used to plenty of solitude, and space. She also knew that Dionne would have no problem telling him to sod off if that was what she wanted, so Lynne decided to give her friend an hour or so in peace.

"Harry, come and help me set the Xbox up and find a good game," said Lynne, holding out her hand to Harry. "Oh, and Di, can you send our coffees down to us in the games room when Connor brings them please."

They walked to the games room. Harry spoke first, "Was Di trying to get rid of me, it certainly felt like it. Or am I being paranoid?"

"Harry, if she wanted you to go, you would be told in no uncertain terms. She can be pretty blunt and bad ass. She'd tell you straight if she was fucking you off. I thought she was quite cute back there."

"Eh? Cute? How?" Harry had no idea what Lynne was on about.

"Ok, how to put this, she is used to hours and hours of solitude every day. She is used to answering to nobody, except me on occasion, and she has been celibate for at least five years. John was pretty sick for the last three years of his life, and I know they suffered issues because of that. So you walk into her life, all gorgeous and virile. You probably knackered her out last night (Harry blushed) and awakened a few emotions that she pushed into an iron box a few years ago. I read her comment back there totally different to you."

Harry considered what Lynne had said. "Ok, how did you read it then?"

"I read it as she wants you to stay, but she is scared of wanting you. There's shit loads of baggage that comes with Di, and my guess is that she thinks you won't want her when you find out just how much. She's not an easy person to get to know, Harry, but keep at it, and cut her some slack."

"I know she's rich Lynne, there's no surprise there. I had figured that much out, even though she was a bit evasive. I'm not exactly a pauper, so neither of us has worries about gold digging." Harry replied sharply.

"Harry, trust me, you have no idea," said Lynne softly." Dan told me you are on ten mill a movie, is that right? So what, twenty mill a year?"

"About that," snapped Harry, a bit uncomfortable.

"She can make that in a morning, it's like falling off a log for her. She likens it to a game of chess. Strategy and planning are her thing."

Harry went cold. "I have no chance with her, have I?" He sighed.

"Yes I think you do. You just need to understand who she is, and what she is, and accept that you are here because she wants you. This is all new to her Harry, she hasn't started a new relationship since she was a teenager, let alone with a bloody sex god. I mean, look at it from her perspective, you have money, you can have any woman you choose, what else does she have that would keep you interested?"

Harry gave Lynne a quick hug. "Thank you. It's what I needed to hear. Now shall we check out these games? Not sure about super mario, I saw call of duty in here earlier. That game is brilliant."

"Mario is the only one she can play, even then she's a bit shit at it," laughed Lynne.

The two of them set up the Xbox, and raked through the games, setting up the easiest one they could find. By the time they had finished, they were firm friends.

Lynne went behind the large bar, "want a beer?" She asked.

"Yeah, please," called out Harry from the large cupboard that housed the DVD collection. Lynne poured out two beers, and together they hunted through the films for something to watch if super mario got too boring that evening.

Dionne finished her emails, and shut down her computer before she was tempted to open the one from Adam Fairchild.

That evening, the four of them ate their roast in the breakfast room, as Dionne thought that the dining room was a bit ott for just the four of them. After their meal, they all flopped onto the sectional sofas in the games room.

Lynne set up a mario contest, which Dan won, and Dionne came last, which Harry thought was cute. Seeing her playing and having a laugh made his heart soar, the intensity of his feelings catching him off guard.

Afterwards, they settled down to watch a film. Lynne had chosen 'Ted', which was a comedy, and Harry snuggled into Dionne to watch it. Towards the end, Harry noticed that Dionne's breathing had become slower and deeper. He looked down at her and realised she had fallen asleep. As the credits rolled, he motioned to the others to stay quiet, and picked her up and carried her to bed. He managed to get her jeans off without waking her, and tucked her into the duvet. Leaving a note on her bedside table, he grabbed his holdall, and after kissing her forehead, left to go home.

He returned to a cold, dark house. He fired up the heating, and made himself a cup of tea. He sat in the familiarity of his own living room ruminating on the weekend's events.

Harry's house was not your typical bachelor pad. It was neat and clean, and very stylishly furnished. He favoured rich, warm colours, and comfortable but modern furniture. He sat and contemplated how it would feel to bring Dionne back there. Apart from his brother's wives, and his cleaner, he had never brought a woman to his house.

He began to worry that he had done the right thing by coming home, feeling the sudden, and unexpected ache of loneliness at not being with her. Pushing those thoughts aside, he made his way up the stairs and into his large, empty bed.

Laying awake, he mulled over the possibility that he was falling in love. It was the first time he yearned for someone, and it had him thinking about all sorts of possibilities. He had always assumed that love was something that happened to other men, and somehow he had been cursed with the inability to connect with a woman. *'Ive got a girlfriend'* the thought hit him, sending a thrill up his spine.

Dionne woke early, and almost instinctually reached over to the other side of the bed. Feeling it cold and empty woke her completely. She sat up and looked round the room. Spotting Harry's note, she read;

Good morning beautiful

You were exhausted last night, so I left you to get a good nights sleep. Could you call me when you have some spare time?

Lots of love

Harry xx

The *'lots of love'* jumped out of the page at her, making her heart quicken slightly, despite the fact she was a bit pissed that he had gone home after all.

'My own bloody fault,' she thought.

After showering and dressing, she headed into her office and switched on the screens. Marion was due in that day, and no doubt Lynne would be over at eight for their latte o'clock.

With some trepidation, she clicked on Adam Fairchild's email to open it.

Background check on Harry Cooper

Prepared by Adam Fairchild for Dionne Devere

Name: Harry William Cooper

DOB: 1/5/1982

Address: 14 Pondbury Gardens, London, SW1

The Beauty & The Blonde

Home tel: 0207 212 4123

Mobile:077890 43856

NI no: H435 1982C

Parents: Ronald Cooper 1949-2007

       Janet Cooper 1954-1988

Siblings: James Cooper insurance underwriter

       Sean Cooper Armed forces

       David Cooper doctor

       Simon Cooper Chef

Salary as per 2011/12 tax return: 17893000.30

Bank accounts:

Barclays, South Kensington branch acc 3370212355 sort 20-17-61

Balance £1340021.75

Abbey national Chelsea branch acc 2908574 balance £33456789.45

Also a maxi ISA containing the maximum £10000.

Other assets: House in Pondbury gardens mortgage free, value approx 3.5 mil.

Car, Aston Martin, value approx £100000

Debt: none

Employment: Actor, under contract to Universal pictures until 2014

Agent is Celebrity Artists. Contracted until 2014 @ 12% of earnings worldwide.

Orientation: Heterosexual/deviant

Previous relationships: no significant relationships found

Current relationships: none found

Dionne read the email at least 3 times, the word 'Deviant' jumping out at her, and swimming in front of her eyes. She made a mental note to call Adam and find out what the hell he meant by it.

Lynne showed up with their lattes at eight. Dionne told her about Adams email. Lynne took a more pragmatic view. "You shagged him yourself Di, you'd know if he was a perv or not. Doesn't strike me as into pain or bondage from what you told me. You could always dress up in leather or rubber and test him out if you're bothered."

"You are really batting for team Harry aren't you?" Challenged Dionne.

"Yup. He's a nice guy, and it's fun watching you go gooey when he's around. I never see you like that. I think he's good for you. Just try not to drive the poor bloke away, eh Di?"

"It's been a long time since I did this Lynne, I am a bit out of practice. Anyway, he may well think I'm a one night stand for all we know."

"You are *so* wrong there, trust me, I know a smitten kitten when I see one. Just go with the flow, and *try* not to put your work first all the time, he will need a lot of reassurance from you that you're interested in him."

Dionne gaped at Lynne, guessing (correctly) that her friend had spoken to Harry. "Ok, I'll trust you here. Can you source me a leather corset, sex toys, some rubber whatever's, and a bloody handbook on 'perversions' please. I'll test out your theory."

"Atta girl," said Lynne. "Marion'll be here any minute, so I'll let you get on, and I'll get over to Soho and search out some goodies. Hide that email from Marion, if I were you." With that, Lynne collected up their cups and left.

Midway through her meeting with Marion, Connor knocked on the door of her office, and entered. "There has been a delivery for you of a personal nature. Security have already checked it" he announced stiffly.

Dionne hurried out to the foyer to see a huge teddy bear with a bouquet of flowers tied into its paws. Her tummy did a delicious flip. She found the card and ripped it open.

Hi beautiful

Thanks for the best weekend ever, hope I can see you again soon

Love H xx

Dionne's face broke into a huge grin, which stayed there all through the endless emails, phone calls and reports that day.

Lynne returned laden with bags, which she took straight up to Dionne's bedroom. Dionne sat on the bed while Lynne pulled sex toys out of bags and explained what to do with them, the pair of them descending into fits of giggles more than a few times.

"Poor Harry won't know what's hit him," giggled Dionne

Meanwhile, Harry descended the steps into a discreet entrance in Belgrave Square. The only clue being a tiny plaque announcing that he was at an establishment called The Chamber. The receptionist was a striking looking brunette who was dressed in a leather catsuit. She greeted him with a wide smile. "Good afternoon Mr Cooper. Is it the usual today?"

"Please," he replied. She pressed an intercom, and announced his arrival. Shortly afterwards, a woman wearing a white tunic appeared, and ushered him through. He followed her down the corridor into a room marked 'The Nursery'. Inside was an enormous cot containing a blue gingham quilt, a couch, tv, and toy box. The woman disappeared, and Harry got changed into a pair of soft, old, superman pyjamas and waited for her return.

She came back carrying a tray which held tiny meat paste

sandwiches and a beaker of squash. She switched on the tv, and loaded up a DVD of cartoons. Harry sat on the floor cross legged watching the cartoons, and eating the curious sandwiches while the woman sat behind him on the couch, out of his line of sight, and stroked his head.

He felt himself starting to relax, really relax, into an almost trance like state. After half an hour, the woman told him to get into the cot. She gave him the beaker of squash in a child's sippy cup, and continued to stroke his hair, murmuring what a sweet boy he was, while Harry slipped his hand down the front of his pyjamas and masturbated. He didn't look at her, his eyes becoming glazed and unseeing. He came quickly, spurting semen over his pyjama top. The woman didn't bat an eyelash, and just cleaned him up with a tissue, and left.

Harry got dressed, put the pyjamas back in his holdall, paid his bill in cash at the front desk, and left feeling a bit ashamed, but relaxed.

He returned home and immediately threw the pyjamas in the wash, repacking his bag with his gym kit. He had a photoshoot the next day for GQ magazine, so planned to hit the gym and pump up his arms a bit.

When he was satisfied with his workout, he showered, and sat in the coffee bar at his gym to cool down and caffeine up. He switched on his mobile, and scrolled through the various texts, stopping at one from Dionne.

Love the flowers and Teddy. Is it wrong that I missed you this morning? Call me when you're free. D xx

The text made him smile, the simple thrill of getting a text from his girlfriend warmed him right through. He decided to call her and see if he could go round there again that evening. He needed to see her again.

She picked up on the second ring. "Hello gorgeous, thanks for the flowers."

"Hello beautiful, and you are more than welcome," replied Harry.

They chatted about their respective days, Harry omitting his trip to

The Chamber, and decided to meet up that evening.

'Yes! Seeing her again.' He thought, pleased with himself for remembering to send the flowers.

Harry arrived at five to seven, using the code for the gates that Dionne had given him. They ate in the breakfast room, a more intimate and seductive dinner than the one they shared the previous night. They talked about the GQ shoot the following day, and Harry's next film, which was going to start shooting in January in LA.

Dionne wrestled with herself before blurting out, "I have a house in LA, you're welcome to stay there. Better than staying at a hotel."

Harry blinked at her, at a loss.

'Of course she's got a house there' he thought.

"That's really kind of you, thank you. I hate staying in hotels. Have you got homes anywhere else?"

She paused for a moment, before answering, "Yeah, um, a couple. There's one in Barbados, one in Switzerland, the LA one, a New York apartment, and a country house here." She blushed, a bit embarrassed.

"Where's the country house here?" Harry asked.

"The Cotswolds, near Upper Slaughter. I rarely use it nowadays, but Lynne loves it. I used to spend the summer there as its fitted out for me to work. We have stables which is the main draw for Lynne. Do you ride?" Harry replied that he loved riding, and would love to see the house.

"Want to go Friday?" asked Dionne.

"Love to." Harry replied.

As things were settled that they would be seeing each other that weekend, both began to relax, although Dionne was getting uncomfortable in the leather corset she was wearing under her dress. It was cinched tight at the waist, and chafed a bit under her arms.

'This better be worth it' she thought to herself.

The conversation moved on to their teenage selves, Harry described his boarding school, keeping her entertained with funny stories. She asked him about his first forays into acting, and how he met Dan.

"Have you ever fallen in love?" She asked, holding her breath.

"I thought so. It was the horrible girl I lost my virginity to. I was like a lovesick puppy. When she was vile to me, I must have looked like a kicked puppy," he laughed. "Apart from her, no, never met anyone I wanted to see more than once."

The significance of those words wasn't lost on Dionne. She found herself wondering if he was feeling as much for her as she felt for him, when he interrupted her musings.

"Have you ever thought about retiring?" He asked the question as he was concerned that her quest for anonymity was going to be at odds with his career.

"Yes, I thought about it after John died, but if I'm honest, working kept me sane, and gave me a focus. There are times, especially when it's stressful, when I feel like selling up and doing a bit of travelling and lazing about." Dionne admitted.

"It just seems a shame not to enjoy the fruits of your labours while you can. I plan to do this job till I'm 40, then get out. Don't want to be one of those ageing film stars who have to wear toupees and corsets," said Harry, shuddering at the thought, and completely oblivious to how much he just insulted Dionne.

She blinked at him, eyes wide. "I'm 40." Harry turned puce red.

"Oh shit, sorry Di, I didn't mean...bugger, I just don't see you as being any different from me. I'm really sorry, I really didn't mean to insult you. Actors age in dog years, so it's different." he scrabbled to backtrack, feeling flustered.

"Calm down," laughed Dionne "I can see the funny side." She was glad the conversation had moved away from the subject of her retirement, although she had been turning the idea over in her mind.

"So, have you given any further thought to the prospect of your sexual adventure?" She asked in a low voice.

"Haven't thought about much else to be honest," admitted Harry," my only caveat is no pain. Yours or mine."

"Agreed," said Dionne, "anything else you don't want to try?"

"No idea," replied Harry, he went on," as long as you're gentle with me, I think I'd try anything once with you."

Dionne took a deep breath, (as much as she could in that blasted corset) "any problems with sex toys?"

"Nope. Never tried them, but I'll give it a go." Harry was starting to twitch, so shifted in his chair.

"Any fears about being restrained? You know, fur handcuffs, things like that?"

"Nope, not with you, I trust you," he replied, noticing her flush. Dionne stood up and held out her hand to him. He stood with her, and allowed himself to be led up to her bedroom.

Dionne undressed him, planting light kisses over each bit of newly exposed skin. He smelt of body wash, and powerful male pheromones, a heady combination. When he was deliciously naked, Dionne pushed him down onto the bed, and pulled two pairs of furry handcuffs from her bedside table. She snapped a pair over each wrist, and attached them to rungs on her iron headboard above his head.

"Is that ok? Are you comfortable?" She asked.

"Yep, all ok, just wondering when you're getting naked," replied Harry, a touch of anxiety in his voice betraying him.

Dionne stood a few feet away from him, and began to strip, slowly, teasing him with the tie of her wrap dress, which was pretty much the only item of clothing she planned to take off. She turned her back to him as she undid it, and slipped it down to reveal a totally bare shoulder. From Harry's vantage point, it looked as though she was naked under her dress. She turned as she shed her dress, to reveal the tightly laced black leather corset, lace thong, black stockings and high heels.

"Jesus Christ, Di, you look so fuckin hot," gasped Harry, pulling on the handcuffs, reflexively wanting to touch her. She sauntered over to him, and bent down over him to kiss him, a deep lush kiss that carried on down his neck, right down his chest, and culminated in her tonguing his nipple while she teased the other with her fingers.

When she could see his cock straining and throbbing, she reached over and picked up some massage oil from the cabinet. It was scented with sandalwood and musk. Earthy, masculine scents, which would arouse the senses. She warmed a little oil in her hands, and massaged his feet, legs and stomach with soft, light strokes. She added a little more oil, and began to stroke his balls, and the sensitive area underneath them, and round to his anus. Harry moaned softly, and lifted his legs as Dionne gently massaged his anus with her finger. With her other hand, she reached over and picked up a small anal vibrator that she had copiously lubed earlier.

Harry's eyes sprung open when she gently inserted it, but he didn't object. She climbed off the bed, and took off her thong. She climbed on to straddle him, but before she sunk onto him, she reached round and switched on the tiny vibrator inside him. The combination of sensations was mindblowing. Harry could only watch helplessly as she slid up and down him. When she pressed another vibrator to her clit, Harry felt the sensation travel down to his dick, making him feel as though his impending orgasm would blow his cock apart.

He watched her working herself to her orgasm, itching to touch her and taste her. He drank in the sight of her in the corset, her nipples peeking over the top of the quarter cut cups. He watched her face for the signs of her impending orgasm.

When she came, it was explosive, rippling and pulsing around his cock, it tipped him well and truly over the edge. Harry screamed as he came, the vibrating butt plug ensuring his orgasm went on and on, spurting hotly, harder than he ever had before. He felt out of control, having to lay helplessly with no way of calming his body. It was the longest, most intense orgasm of his life.

Dionne turned off the vibrators, and pulled Harry's one out. She unlocked the handcuffs, and rubbed his shoulders as he enveloped her in a hug.

"Did I hurt you baby?" She asked, "You screamed, and it worried me."

"No, it was a huge orgasm, not painful, just surprising," he replied."I'm just glad my dicks still in one piece, I thought you were gonna blow it apart back there."

"So you like the corset then?" she winked coquettishly.

"You look sensational, one for the wank bank most definitely, and you smell like a new car." He smiled, and they both laughed.

"Not quite the effect I was aiming for," she giggled. "Can you help me out of it please, it's bloody uncomfortable."

"Must have been hell trying to eat wearing that, I just thought you weren't hungry this evening," laughed Harry, as he undid the laces at the back, tracing little kisses down her spine.

When she was naked, he pulled her into his arms and held her tight. "Thank you for that," he breathed,"it was a revelation, I've never screamed before, well not in a good way."

The two lovers fell asleep facing one another, holding each other tightly.

CHAPTER 6

The next morning they both awoke early, and shared a leisurely orgasm each before they got up. After breakfast, Harry kissed Dionne goodbye before leaving for his photoshoot.

Dionne wandered into her office. Her heart wasn't in it. The thought of spending the day glued to a screen made her heart sink.

'*Maybe it's time to stop*' she thought.

Lynne arrived at 8 with their lattes.

"Do you think it's time for me to give up working?" Dionne asked her.

Lynne pondered the question, before replying, "yes, if its what you want. If it doesn't excite you anymore, then quitting at the top is always a good strategy. If it's what someone else wants, then no, you'd resent him for it."

"I'm depressed at the thought of spending all day in this office. I've been bored with it for a while, I just didn't have anything else going on before." Dionne admitted.

"Then it's time to sell," said Lynne." It's a big wide world out there. By the way how did the perv thing go?"

"Nearly blew his cock off," admitted Dionne. The pair of them dissolved into laughter.

"Poor Harry, bet he didn't know what had hit him," snorted Lynne.

"He still looked at bit dazed this morning," laughed Dionne.

Still laughing, Lynne gathered up their cups, while Dionne told her they would be going to the country house that weekend. She spent the morning organising transport and informing staff of their plans, then decided to call Adam Fairchild.

"Hi Adam, got the background check you sent, but what did you mean by the word 'deviant'?"

"It means he is a member of a sex club called The Chamber in Belgravia, but there is no evidence of why, what he uses it for, or of him paying for any services there using his credit or debit cards. He appears on the members list though." Adam replied.

"Ok, keep me posted if anything comes to light please Adam."

"Will do, speak soon," said Adam, before ending the call.

Dionne made the decision to stop buying assets, and sell anything a buyer approached her for, with the exceptions of her studio shares, the tech company, and her personal homes. She began by releasing some small tranches of stocks for sale, nothing that would arouse suspicion, but enough to allow her to close one of her myriad holding companies.

She met Douggie at the Wolsley for lunch. Douggie was on good form, and she began to enjoy herself. After dessert, he came to the point of why he had asked to see her.

"I have a party interested in acquiring land in Scotland, a lot of land, particularly around both Aberdeen and Edinburgh. What sort of holdings have you got that you would be willing to sell?" He asked quietly, so they wouldn't be overheard.

"I have significant amounts, you know that already, but the geology reports indicate possible oil deposits in the area around Aberdeen. You know I'm not going to sell it for tuppence. I know what it's worth to the oil industry." Dionne was playing hardball.

"Shell have expressed an interest. They want to make you an offer once they know the exact acreage, and position. Mobil may also be interested too. With the Edinburgh land, I have a local developer interested in four sites that are registered to you. So I thought I would personally find out how resistant you are to selling before putting proposals together." Douggie looked at her expectantly.

"Happy to sell Edinburgh, as long as the buyer takes all six sites I own there. As for the rest, well there is at least a million acres around Aberdeen and its surroundings, but put to your buyers that I know the value, so they better make their offers sensible." Dionne looked him squarely in the eye, knowing if this deal came off, most of the land she owned in Scotland would be gone.

They agreed that Dionne would email him the land details, and Douggie would come back to her with the offers.

Dionne returned home, content with her decisions, and excited to discuss her day with Harry, knowing he would be pleased at her resolution to scale back her workload.

She found the information that Douggie had asked for, and emailed it to him. She then released all of her holding of Japanese junk bonds for sale, prompting a phone call from Darren.

"Are you trying to fuck over Japan?" He bellowed down the phone.

"Don't be daft, I sold a load of currency at the same time to counter, if you had bothered to look you moron," countered Dionne, glad to be leaving the world of Darren Karrett at some point.

"Hmm, I always think you're up to no good, why are you doing this?" He demanded.

"Getting out of junk bonds, Darren, too complex, and too much work for my eensy weensey brain to process."

"Don't lie to me. God you're an annoying woman. If you want out, I'll buy what you got, at 80% of market value of course," said Darren. Dionne could tell he was smirking, even down the phone.

"Too late. Sold the lot. Got a good price too. Listen, I did you a favour, the price has plummeted now, you should fill your boots." Laughing, she cut the call, knowing that Darren's holding was worth 75% of what it was that morning.

Harry was in a studio in Chelsea being styled for a photoshoot. He sat patiently while the stylist straightened his hair and sponged makeup over his face. The photographers assistant took ages fiddling with the lighting. He used the time to contemplate how he felt about the recent changes in his life. He could picture himself with Dionne, coming home to her every night, sharing insights and secrets, except, that secret. Harry thought about giving up his visits to The Chamber, and wondered how long he could go before needing it. He resolved to stop going, to see if he could. Without The Chamber in the equation, he figured sharing his life with Dionne would be a lot less complicated.

The photographer pulled him back to reality by barking orders at him to change pose, which Harry dutifully complied with, hoping the shoot would be over quickly.

Harry scrubbed the makeup off his face before he left the studio, and headed straight over to Dionne's. When he arrived, he learnt that Dionne was in the library. She was curled up in one of the squashy armchairs reading a book about sexual techniques, which she attempted to hide when Harry walked in. He pulled it out from under her, and scanned the title.

"Hey, there's me thinking you were a natural," he teased. "Now I find out you know marginally more than me, you're just getting ideas from a book."

Dionne blushed. "Okay, you caught me. I'll let you read it after me. Why is your hair like that?" she eyed him, curious.

"Photoshoot. They wanted me with straight hair. No idea why. I washed the makeup off before I came over though. Felt like I was wearing a mask. So how was your day?" Harry leaned over her to give her a quick kiss before she answered.

"It's been eventful. Sit down, and I'll organise a drink, then I'll tell you all about it."

"Sounds exciting. Could I have a beer please?" said Harry, intrigued.

Dionne ordered their drinks, then settled back into her chair, staring into the fire. "I began selling off assets today. Probably means very little to you, but it's a big decisive turning point for me. I aim to cash in most of my assets over the next couple of years. It means I stop dealing, or trading, which ultimately means I stop working, and start living." She pulled her gaze from the flames, and over to Harry, and found him smiling at her.

"If that's a decision you're happy with Di, then I'm delighted. If you are doing this for any other reason than your own happiness, then I urge you to think carefully. I can't claim to really understand exactly what you're telling me, or what it involves, but I just want you to find contentment." Harry held her gaze as he spoke, his words making her heart leap.

Dionne paused a while before she spoke. "Contentment would right now be having the freedom to enjoy the next two months off with you, maybe a holiday, without having one eye on a screen, that's if you want me around," she added quickly.

Harry knelt in front of her chair and drew her into a hug. "I would love you around for the next two months, and beyond, and I would love to take you somewhere fabulous for a holiday, and have you to myself." He scanned her face anxiously, worried in case he was being over keen.

"It's a deal. Two months of no work, apart from me signing papers to sell stuff, and you doing your contractual stuff," smiled Dionne.

"Deal," he grinned.

They decided to go out and celebrate. Harry managed to get a table at Nobu, which pleased Dionne enormously. She discovered that she enjoyed being out and about with him, rather than hidden in her fortress.

They sat and made their plans for the two months off they had pencilled in. They discussed spending Christmas together in the Cotswolds or Switzerland, and decided on a trip to Barbados early December.

"Only problem with spending Christmas together is what the hell I'm going to buy you," laughed Harry. "I'll have to enlist Lynne's help with that one," he smiled.

"I can think of loads of things I'd like to buy you," teased Dionne.

"I know something I'd like us to do in our time off," Harry ventured, "I'd like you to come back to my place and spend the night. I've never taken a woman home, and never shared my bed. I'd like you to be the first."

Dionne was surprised. "Never? Well I would be honoured. Just clear security with Craig and tell me when. I'd love to see your house," she said.

By the time they left the restaurant, Dionne was a bit tipsy, and Harry was pleasantly buzzing. They fell into bed giggling, deciding on just a quickie, with a more vigorous session planned for the morning.

Dionne awoke with Harry pushing into her from behind. "Morning sexy," she purred." This is now my most favourite way to wake up."

Harry flipped her onto her back and shifted on top of her. He pushed in again, and began to move at a faster, more primal pace, as if he was trying to climb inside her. As he pounded her, she felt the familiar quickening, as he relentlessly drove her towards her orgasm. She came with a strangled cry, her back arching off the bed. He plunged into her one last time before his own orgasm shook his body.

'I'm getting good at this,' he thought, smugly.

He rolled off her, and lay beside her as he caught his breath. After a while, when their breathing had slowed, he turned to her, and gazed into her eyes.

"Dionne, what I feel for you scares me," he admitted.

She saw the emotion in his face," me too," she told him. He kissed her gently, caressing her face, before burying his face in her neck, and holding her tightly.

They showered together, Dionne washed his hair, delighted that his curls returned, and he soaped her all over before lifting her up and making love to her against the wall of the shower.

"You're insatiable" asserted Dionne afterwards.

"Are you complaining?" He asked

"No, just an observation." she smirked.

"It's you. You just turn me on by simply existing. I can't seem to keep my hands off you." He proved his point by tweaking her nipples, which made her laugh.

"Harry, you're turning into a sex fiend. I've created a monster."

Harry followed her into her dressing room and watched her get dressed.

"What's through that door?" he asked, pointing to a doorway at the far end of her walk in wardrobe.

"Jewellery room. Want to see?" She replied. She punched a code into the keypad beside the door, and pushed it open. Harry followed her in. The small room was fitted out with narrow drawered chests, almost like museum chests, only these were modern looking and made of pale oak. Dionne slid out a drawer to reveal an internal fitting like a jewellery shop one, holding a diamond pendant, matching earrings, and a matching bracelet. She indicated that Harry could look in the drawers. He opened one and gasped at the enormous ruby set he uncovered.

"Scratch jewellery off the list for Christmas," he said quietly, overawed by the size of the rubies he was looking at." Do all these drawers contain stuff like this?"

"Yes they do," admitted Dionne."The existence of this room is a secret Harry, only Lynne knows the full extent of my collection, and now you. It's not something I want to be public knowledge."

"Don't blame you. Is it safe here?" He asked, "there must be millions in here."

"The room is steel lined. It also doubles as a safe room in case of attack."

"Good to know. This is unreal Di, it's like the bloody Crown Jewels."

Dionne paused, and took a breath. "I wanted you to know who I am, what I am. I need to be able to be honest with you, and to be able to trust you."

"I would never hurt you, or place you in danger Di, never worry about that."

They left the room, and while Dionne did her makeup, Harry got dressed, each quietly contemplating the level of trust building in their growing relationship.

Lynne came over at eight, and finding Dionne's office empty, hunted her down in the breakfast room. The three of them sat sipping coffee while they discussed plans for the two months. It was decided that Lynne would remain in London during their Barbados trip, as she had some social events she didn't want to miss, but she would spend Christmas in the Cotswolds with them, and invite Dan to join them too. It was also decided that Lynne needed to shop for the Barbados trip for Harry, as well as Dionne, and that she would organise a pre-holiday spa day for the three of them.

Harry wanted to get Lynne alone to discuss what Dionne would like for Christmas. He knew it would make him anxious until he had a firm idea of what to do. When Dionne nipped to the bathroom, he seized his chance.

"What on earth am I going to get her for Christmas?" He asked Lynne.

"There's loads of things she likes, don't worry, I'll help you." Lynne dismissed the question with a wave.

"Such as?" Demanded Harry, determined not to be fobbed off.

"She likes nice bath stuff, clothes, shoes, loads of stuff," said Lynne, smiling at him.

'You really are a smitten kitten' she thought.

"Ok, I'll take you shopping. Pencil me into your diary," pouted Harry.

Harry sat with Dionne in her office while she answered her emails. The offers had come in from Douggie, which were decent enough to make Dionne raise her eyebrows, before accepting them, subject to an uplift clause. Harry was trying to read over her shoulder, but couldn't work out the number of zeros fast enough to get a handle on how much was at stake. Dionne quickly briefed her lawyer on the deal, and gave Marion a string of instructions. Then she was free for the day.

They started off by going over to Harry's house, which Dionne was deeply impressed with. She admired his taste, declared that she loved his kitchen, and let him fuck her enthusiastically on his bed.

He packed some clothes into a case, turned off the heating, and headed back to Dionne's.

They spent the following couple of days lounging around, swimming, and watching TV. Neither of them feeling the need for the outside world. Lynne was preoccupied with her growing relationship with Dan, so wasn't around much.

Friday morning, Dionne briefed her PA, replied to a couple of emails and signed a few documents, before racing out to the waiting Bentley. Harry had assumed they would be driven to the Cotswolds, and was shocked when they pulled into Battersea heliport.

"You got a helicopter?" He enquired.

"No, I wouldn't use it enough, I just hire one when I need it. There's a helipad at the house that was there when I bought it, so it's convenient to fly down."

They were shown into a large helicopter, which Harry assumed was a luxury version, and sat while the pilot did his checks. They took off gracefully, following the curve of the Thames as they headed west.

After what seemed too short a time to appreciate the breathtaking views, the helicopter landed neatly in the grounds of a country estate. As the rotors powered down, Harry took in his surroundings. The house was just visible behind a hill. It looked Georgian, like a stately home.

They got out of the chopper, and Dionne led him to the house. As they approached, the front door swung open, held by a tiny, dark haired woman who was smiling broadly.

"Welcome back ma'am, sir," she said.

"Thank you Janice, and this is Harry," said Dionne, stepping aside to allow Harry to shake Janice's hand. "This is Janice, she takes care of this house with her husband Terry," explained Dionne.

"Harry Cooper, the film star?" Gasped Janice.

"That's me," answered Harry, giving her his best knicker combusting smile. She immediately blushed and giggled.

"So excited to meet you, enjoy your stay," she replied in a breathy voice. Dionne rolled her eyes and grabbed Harry's hand, proceeding to give him a guided tour. The house was much larger than her London home, just as beautifully furnished, but in a more country style, leaning more towards comfort than impeccable styling.

She briefly showed him the vast gardens, which, although it was winter, still looked beautiful with topiary and a large evergreen knot garden. She explained that the house had 70 acres of gardens, including a large lake, and the stables.

They had lunch in the conservatory, after which they took a walk around the lake, holding hands and stopping every now and then to steal kisses.

"It's so nice not having your security trailing behind us," mused Harry.

"Oh, they're here, they did a sweep before we arrived, but the whole house and grounds are extremely secure here, so I do get a bit more privacy. Do the security crew bother you?" She asked, frowning slightly.

"I'm just aware of talking in front of them, and I feel sad for you that you have to have them all the time."

"I'm barely aware of them most of the time. I need them more in London. I feel safer here, although I'm probably not," she laughed."You probably need them more than me. Janice looked like she wanted to eat you alive. I love watching women go all silly over you," she stated, her lips quirking up.

"It's only a pretty face. They probably think I look taller on the telly," he teased.

"You do look taller on telly, and it's a very pretty face, connected to an extremely sexy man," said Dionne, squeezing his bum.

"Careful, or you'll get twigs up your bottom when I shag you right here," laughed Harry. They spent the rest of the afternoon exploring the gardens.

The following day they decided to look around the local villages. They wandered round little antique shops and tourist stores before trying out a tiny tea shop with Craig squashed into a table behind them. The waitress brought them a pot of tea, some pretty teacups and a plate of tiny sandwiches. Dionne lifted the pot

"Shall I be mother?" She asked. She watched Harry carefully as he went pale, and looked as though he was trying to control his breathing."Are you ok?" She asked, wondering what was wrong. He took a few deep breaths, and dragged his eyes back to Dionne.

"Yeah, flashback type of thing," he muttered.

"Flashback to what?" She asked softly.

"When my mum was alive. I was six when she died, so I have some memories. Every now and then, one slaps me round the face. Would you mind either eating the sandwiches quick or getting rid of them please Di?"

She took the plate and put it down in front of Craig at the next table, out of Harry's view. "Is that better?" She asked, puzzled.

"Yeah, it's fine now thanks, sorry," apologised Harry, feeling a bit ashamed. He called the waitress back over and ordered a couple of cakes for Dionne.

They sat in silence, Dionne trying to fathom out what had just happened, and Harry wrestling with how to tell her.

"Do you want to share this with me?" Enquired Dionne.

Harry looked her squarely in the eyes. "Ok, but it sounds weird. When I was small, my mum used to do what she called dolly sandwiches for tea sometimes, and it takes me back to a time when I was safe and happy. Then she died. It was just strange for me seeing you and her in the same place. I'm not explaining it well."

Dionne's heart broke for him. She stroked his hand, "do you often think of her?" She asked softly.

"Not often. More so since I met you I suppose."

Dionne frowned, "why's that?"

"Because after my mum died, I never got close to a woman again, until you." Harry wanted to say the 'L' word, but held back, feeling it wasn't the right moment.

"Oh," said Dionne, unsure of how to respond. The whole episode putting a seed of doubt in her head *'am I a mother figure?'* ran through her mind. She pushed those thoughts aside, and concentrated on his beautiful face, scanning him, trying to read his emotions.

He sipped his tea. "You're nothing like her Di, she was a tall brunette who could barely read and write, not a dainty blonde with a mind like a supercomputer. Please don't ever think I'm looking for a mother substitute in you, I'm not." He had an uncanny ability to read her mind, which at that moment, she was grateful for.

"Glad to hear it," she replied, still unsure how to handle his revelations.

They finished their tea, and headed back to the car. Harry slipped his arm around her shoulders as they walked, holding her close. She slid her hand into the back pocket of his jeans, and enjoyed the closeness, and feeling his body heat.

Back at the house, she asked him what he wanted to do that evening. He blushed before answering.

"What I always want to do with you," he said sporting a boyish grin. "I want to carry on my adventure. By the way I thought of something I'd like to try, if you're game that is," he added quickly. Before she could answer, he drew her into a deep, passionate kiss.

He led her upstairs to the bedroom, and locked the door. She felt a momentary pang of anxiety as he pulled the furry handcuffs out of his holdall. He placed them on the bedside table, and began to undress her.

"What are you going to do?" She whispered, suddenly unsure. Harry didn't answer, he just carried on undressing her. When she was naked, he gently pushed her onto the bed, and fastened the handcuffs on her wrists, the opposite ends he attached to the bedstead. He leaned over and kissed her again, before trailing little kisses down her neck, not stopping until he reached her nipple.

"I want to watch you come. I felt it, but I've never seen it," he breathed, before clambering off the bed and stripping out of his clothes. He disappeared into Dionne's dressing room and returned a few moments later with two dressing gown ties, which he proceeded to tie round her ankles. He then tied the other ends around around the bottom legs of the bed, so she was totally spread eagled. He grabbed the vibrator from the nightstand before crawling up from the bottom of the bed, so he was nestled between her outspread legs.

He began by stroking her gently with his fingers, before parting her completely and sucking softy on her clit. Dionne began to writhe on the bed. The new, dominant Harry was just so unexpected, and rather hot. She closed her eyes to let the sensations wash over her. She bucked when he inserted two fingers inside her to massage her g spot, slowly sliding them in and out. She heard the vibrator click on, and turned up to full speed. Harry brought it up to touch her clit while continuing to stroke her g spot with his fingers.

"Is that what you like?" he asked hoarsely. Dionne could only garble a reply before she climaxed with a scream. Being unable to close her legs made the orgasm go on and on. Harry watched with rapt attention as she pulsed around his fingers. Seeing her orgasm for himself turned him on so much, he thought he would come there and then.

When she began to recover from her climax, she became aware of Harry shifting. He moved up the bed, over her, and in a quick motion, shoved his cock inside her.

He only gave one thrust before shouting "fuck," as he spurted inside her.

He collapsed on top of her, unusually careless about his weight, until her muffled shouts alerted him to the fact that she was struggling to breathe. He pulled off her and perched on the side of the bed.

"I like you tied up," he said with an impassive expression that made Dionne feel a bit uncomfortable.

"Not my favourite thing," she replied, scanning his face.

"Made you scream though," smiled Harry, looking pleased with himself.

He untied her feet, and unlocked the handcuffs. Her shoulders felt stiff, the muscles aching from being held in position, so she decided on a hot bath. Dionne slipped on a robe, and ran a bath, adding her favourite Jo Malone bath oil. While it was running, Harry padded into the bathroom.

"Are you ok? You seem very quiet," he asked.

Dionne had to think about it. She was strangely disquieted, but couldn't articulate why.

'Was it the mother incident in the tea shop or the show of dominance tying me up?' She wondered. "Yeah, I'm fine, just a bit stiff," she replied, not sure how Harry would react if she told him the truth.

Dionne stepped into the bath and immediately felt the soothing effect of the hot water.

"Scoot forward and I'll join you," said Harry, appearing not to notice her disquiet. She moved forward, and he got in behind her, pulling her back against his chest. They both lay for a while, not speaking. Dionne could feel the steady beat of his heart against her back.   Harry spoke first "So you didn't like being tied up?"

"Not really."

"Any reason why?"

"Nope."

Given that women were a mystery to Harry at the best of times, he had no idea how to fathom out why she had gone so arctic on him. She felt his heartbeat speed up, and knew she was making him anxious.

She began to try and articulate why she was feeling off balance. "The thing is, it made me nervous being restrained, and you seemed so dominant, which I'm not used to, and, and...." She stopped, realising she wasn't making sense.

"It turned me on seeing you helpless," said Harry suddenly, "but if you didn't like it, we won't do it again, we are just trying stuff out, remember? I don't want to upset you, I just wanted to try it." She turned to face him. His eyes were round and full of anxiety. She kissed him softly, then more deeply. When she felt him relax, she pulled away from him and turned to sit back down.

"The least you could do is rub my shoulders after you made them ache," she teased. Harry obediently rubbed her shoulders before pulling her into his chest and hugging her tightly.

They lay there awhile, Harry absentmindedly caressing her. When the water started cooling, Dionne got out and wrapped herself in a large towel. She held a fluffy bath sheet out for him, enveloping him as he shivered slightly. He sat on the edge of the bath to watch Dionne apply her body lotion, drinking in the sight of her naked.

"Can I help you?" She smiled, aware he was ogling her.

"You're gorgeous, did you know that?" He said, his face serious.

"Glad you think so. I think you're gorgeous too, so that's lucky." She laughed.

They got into bed to watch TV, Dionne snuggling close while Harry flicked through the channels before settling on a comedy panel show. They watched for a while until Harry realised that Dionne's breathing had slowed and deepened. He gently tucked the covers around her, and leaning up on his elbow, watched her sleep.

CHAPTER 7

They headed back to London the following day. With only a few days before their trip to Barbados, the agenda was shopping and beauty treatments in preparation. Harry discovered just how good a stylist Lynne was, as she effortlessly organised a holiday wardrobe for him.

During one of their shopping expeditions, Harry tried to pump Lynne for information about Dionne.

"What sort of things did John buy Dionne, you know, as a present?" Harry asked.

Lynne laughed. "John was a gazillionaire Harry, he bought her the Elizabeth Taylor diamond one year for her birthday. I doubt very much that Dionne would expect that type of thing from you. Anyway, we're here to concentrate on you today. How resistant are you to colourful shirts?" She said, rifling through a rail of acidic coloured tshirts, before picking out a few for him to try on.

They paused at the chocolate cafe in Harrods for a sit down and a drink.

"A few more pairs of shorts, and some sunglasses and we're done," announced Lynne. Harry thought about the nine thousand quid he had already spent, and the prospect of spending more, and felt very profligate.

"How much are the ball gowns you buy for Di?" He asked.

"About thirty thousand each, although some can be a little more if there's a lot of altering to do, or if they have specialist beading or embroidery. They are usually made for her, but sometimes I buy off the peg and get it altered," said Lynne, without guile, as if it was the most normal thing in the world.

Harry gulped. *'Scratch that off the list too'* he thought.

Lynne had booked Harry a haircut in the urban retreat. What she neglected to mention was that she had also booked him a hot shave and face massage as well. She dropped him off there, and cheerfully told him she would be busy shopping for a few bits for Dionne while he was being attended to, and that she would pick him up in an hour and a half.

Harry found that he thoroughly enjoyed the shave and facial. He asked the hairstylist for a light trim, and was pleased with the result. He came out of the salon to find Lynne   waiting for him in the reception area, surrounded by bags, which Harry arranged to be taken to the car, while he whizzed down to the food hall to pick up some provisions. He had given Craig his spare keys that morning to check his house over, as he planned to cook for Dionne that night.

They returned to the house to find Dionne in her office doing something on her computer. She stopped as soon as Harry and Lynne appeared.

"What have you been buying?" Dionne smiled.

"Loads," said Lynne, and propelled Dionne upstairs to her dressing room where Connor had placed the bags. She pulled some bikinis out of a carrier to show Dionne.

"Gorgeous" said Dionne, "I love the colours."

The pair raked through all the bags while Harry sat and watched. When they were done, he invited Dionne back to his place, promising to cook for her.

They took Harry's car back to south Kensington, battling through the rush hour traffic. He parked neatly outside his house so that Dionne's security could park on his drive, and pulled the bags out of his car. He took Dionne through to his kitchen, and sat her at the marble island so they could talk while he cooked.

Harry was a fairly competent cook. Having to learn at a young age how to take care of himself had spawned an interest in good food. He poured them each a glass of wine and began to chop vegetables. Dionne watched intently, loving the normality of it. She was deeply impressed at how fluidly he moved around his kitchen, finding herself getting turned on just watching him.

He served caviar with blinis and creme fraiche while they were waiting for their beef Wellington to cook. Harry let her feed him the little piles of caviar and blini while he prepared a red wine gravy for their beef, sucking on her fingers, which made her tummy clench in a delicious way.

"You're very good at seductive food play," she purred.

"You just wait till desert," murmured Harry, giving her his best enticing look.

They ate at the kitchen island, enjoying a bottle of Chateaux Margaux with their beef. Harry told her about his day out with Lynne, making Dionne laugh with his description of the indignities she had subjected him to in her quest for the perfect holiday shorts.

"She told me one pair made my bulge look too big. I was mortified that she was even looking," he muttered, blushing at the memory.

Dionne burst out laughing, "Lynne is outrageously blunt, but she will always tell you it's for your own good. She probably thought film star face plus accentuated bulge would equal mobs of rabid women," sniggered Dionne.

For desert, Harry brought out a cheesecake laden with fresh strawberries and whipped cream that he had cheated, and bought from the patisserie department in Harrod's food hall. He held a forkful up to

Dionne's mouth. She let him feed her, groaning as she got a full hit of strawberry. They fed each other, the anticipation building with every mouthful.

Afterwards, he led her to his room, kissing her deeply, revelling in the novelty of having her in his home.

They shared a bath in his expansive ensuite. Harry massaged her feet till she moaned in pleasure.

"That feels so good it should be illegal," she purred.

When she was so relaxed she was almost limp, Harry dried them both and led her to bed. They began by making love slowly and languidly, both enjoying the sensation of their damp bodies sliding over one another. Harry could feel her getting more and more aroused until he felt the now familiar fluttering sensation. He withdrew and flipped her over onto her front. Pulling her hips up, he entered her from behind, rubbing his hands over her beautiful behind as he resumed his rhythm. He reached round and found her clit, massaging tiny circles as he had seen her do before.

Dionne surrendered to the divine sensation, her body building up to a huge climax, as the head of Harry's large penis rubbed her G spot in just the right way. She detonated around him with a scream, feeling him let go a few seconds later. They collapsed onto the bed, slick with sweat.

When Dionne had got her breath back, she turned to him, "Enjoying sex in your bed?"

"Love it," exclaimed Harry, his dick still tingling.

Harry switched on the TV opposite his bed, and they snuggled down to watch the news, which was all about the worsening economic crisis.

"Do you ever worry about being poor?" Asked Harry.

"Um, no, it's not possible," replied Dionne.

"Even if the banks went bust?" He kept on.

"I have diamonds and gold remember?" smiled Dionne, anxious to shut down the conversation.

She ran her hand down the firm ridges of his stomach muscles, not touching his cock as she didn't want to make him flinch. She kissed his ear, running her tongue down his neck.

"I know what I'd like to do in your bed," she breathed, seductively.

"Oh, what's that then?"

"I want you to come in my mouth."

Harry groaned and pulled the covers down to show Dionne what her words alone had done to him. She ran her tongue over his erection, softly and slowly taking him in her mouth. Wrapping her fingers around the shaft, she worked her mouth over the wide crest until she could tell he was close. He had his eyes closed, his hands grasping at the sheet as she paid total attention to his cock. She didn't miss a beat as he came with a shout, spurting hotly into her mouth, and watching wide eyed as she swallowed every drop.

"Doesn't that taste disgusting?" He asked, curious.

"It tastes of you, how could that possibly be anything but delicious?" She smiled.

"Liar, but thank you for the illusion." He kissed the tip of her nose. Inside he was reeling from the revelation that he could enjoy oral sex.

Dionne snuggled into his arms, and breathing in his lovely masculine scent, she promptly fell asleep.

Harry lay in the dark, committing the evening to memory, trying to understand his own feelings. He knew he was in love with her, and he suspected she had feelings for him, but he also realised she was holding something back, and that her life was complex. He was used to the opportunist women who threw themselves at him, but with Dionne, he knew he would be considered the gold digger. The mere thought of it made him uncomfortable.

'It's not like I ask her to buy me anything' he thought.

The following day they left for Barbados. Dionne had arranged a private jet from London City airport, which they both agreed, beat schlepping over to Heathrow. They arrived in Barbados late afternoon local time, a car meeting them to take them straight to the house.

They were driven up a long winding driveway, through enormous gates, towards a huge white villa. It overlooked a white sand beach which resembled a scene from 'South Pacific', palm trees swaying gently in the soft breeze. The gardens were a lush, tropical oasis, surrounding a large pool which glinted in the strong sunlight.

The house was an interior designers dream, all cream with black accents. The furnishings, looking pristine and unused, were a touch impersonal, but extremely stylish.

After Harry had been introduced to the staff, Dionne showed him around while their bags were being unpacked. They found cold beers in the bar by the pool, and kicking off their shoes, walked along the beach. Harry loved seeing Dionne doing normal, carefree stuff, away from the controlled, rarefied London existence she inhabited.

Later that evening, after showering and changing into shorts and vests, they ate outside on the terrace. Dionne had plugged in her iPod, so the soft strains of Eva Cassidy filled the sultry atmosphere of the Caribbean night.

As they shared a bottle of cold, crisp, white wine, Harry decided the moment was right.

"I have something to tell you," he murmured.

"You can tell me anything," replied Dionne, seeing the anxiety on his face.

"I've fallen in love with you," Harry whispered, suddenly unsure of himself.

Dionne stared at him, drinking in his beautiful, anxious face, processing his words, which echoed her own thoughts.

"I've fallen in love with you too," she whispered back to him.

They grinned at each other, before Harry lifted his glass, "To love," he said, as they clinked glasses and drank."I never thought this would happen to me." Harry beamed, leaning over to plant a chaste kiss on Dionne's lips. She paused a beat before kissing him back, deepening it until they were ravishing each other's mouths, trying to communicate their feelings through the kiss.

The next day, they lounged around the pool, swimming, reading and talking. Harry had asked Dionne to explain the financial crisis, which she had done in an easy and precise way that underlined to him her deep understanding of high finance, and it's surrounding politics.

"You're very intelligent," he said.

"My intellect is my defining feature I think. Although it bothers people at times. Maths is probably where I excel," she replied.

"Really? Ok what's one thousand two hundred and sixty seven times thirty four?" Harry teased.

"Forty three thousand and seventy eight," replied Dionne without pausing.

Harry gaped at her, his mouth dropping open. "Wow Di, that's astounding. How do you do that?" He checked her answer on the calculator app on his iPhone.

"I just can. That's what I mean, it bothers some people. Imagine trying to do a deal with me. No matter how much you try, you couldn't get one over on me. It pisses people off a lot. But I can't act for toffee, and my singing sounds like a cat in pain, so you got one over me there."

"That's something I suppose. Even so Di, yours is quite some talent. Is there a limit to your maths abilities, I mean can you calculate the big numbers that quick?" He asked, intrigued.

"Oh yes. I have to stop and think a bit when I do square roots in the billion numbers," she laughed, "but apart from that, no not really."

Dionne went back to her novel, and Harry sat and considered their conversation. He had never contemplated how sexy intelligence could be. He wondered at his good fortune in finding her.

Dionne peered at him over the top of her book, spotting his erection, she teased, "how long would it take of me doing my billion times table to make you come?" She winked at him.

He groaned. "That is so fucking sexy, meet me in the pool."

She squealed and threw her book down. "Last one in has to do sums," as they both jumped in.

They spent the following couple of days either lazing by the pool or making love.

On the fourth day, Harry suggested a trip into Bridgetown to explore. They wandered round the little boutiques and the jewellery shops which catered for the cruise ship crowd, the windows full of gaudy pieces to attract American shoppers. Their security trailed along behind them, casually dressed in pale linen suits which hid their gun holsters. Harry felt a little sorry for them wearing jackets in the stifling heat.

Wandering around the docks Dionne stopped and stared at a vast, elegant super yacht called 'The Pied Piper' moored near the entrance. She pulled out her iPhone and scrolled through her contacts, tapping one.

"James? Hi, it's Dionne. Are you in Barbados? I'm standing by your boat," she paused, listening to the other person. She looked up to wave at a man standing on the deck with a phone pressed to his ear. "Come on Harry, there's a friend of mine I'd like you to meet." She grasped Harry's hand and pulled him towards the gangplank.

James Rankin was a handsome man. With a boyish, almost pretty face, and dirty blonde hair, he had the type of looks which stopped women dead in their tracks. Coupled with a tanned, muscular physique and a devastating smile, the total effect was dazzling. Harry eyed him slightly suspiciously, smiling carefully as Dionne made introductions.

"James, darling, how lovely to see you, this is my boyfriend Harry. Harry this is James Rankin, he's another financier, and an old friend," said Dionne, kissing James on both cheeks.

James shook Harry's hand. "Harry Cooper?" James asked, smiling widely. When Harry nodded his head, James went on, "the bosses boyfriend? Smart move Harry. Heard you bought universal Di. What else are you up to these days?"

Noting that Harry hadn't reacted to James' insult, Dionne explained that they were there for a holiday, and she was taking some time out.

At James insistence they joined him on deck for a drink. From the conversation, Harry worked out that they had been friends for many years. He also worked out that James fancied the pants off of Dionne.

'You can look all you want asshole, she's taken' Harry thought.

Dionne and James gossiped about the markets, people they knew in London, and how badly the banks were behaving. Harry's ears pricked up when he heard Dionne ask,

"So do you have a girlfriend James?"

"My current bimbo is an easy on the eye lingerie model. Her name's Christina. If you come to my party tonight, you can meet her. No long words though Di, or she won't understand." He laughed at his own joke. Harry winced.

James had already invited them to a 'soirée' he was holding that evening on board his yacht.

'Great' thought Harry, after having taken an instant dislike to the man.

They said their goodbyes, promising to come back at eight that evening.

"He fancies you," asserted Harry.

"He fancies anything female, the dozier the better usually. Besides, I'm taken." Dionne said, squeezing Harry's hand.

They got back to the house at six, Dionne's housekeeper had managed to source a hairdresser to do Dionne's hair for the party that evening. Harry sat on the bed and watched as Dionne got ready. She chose a halter neck maxi dress by Versace in bright blues, and a pair of wedge heeled sandals. Harry wore chinos and a loose linen shirt.

"Do I look ok?" Dionne asked as she put the finishing touches to her makeup.

"Like a goddess as always," smiled Harry, looking forward to showing her off.

Harry ushered her out the door and into the car, anxious not to be late. As they pulled up at the dock, they could see people streaming up the gangplank onto James' yacht.

"Looks like lots of people attending," mused Harry, relieved that they wouldn't be stuck with James all evening. They walked onto the boat, taking a glass of champagne each from a waiter.

"Dionne, darling, Harry, hello, welcome to the party," bellowed James, striding over to them. He greeted Dionne with a kiss to both cheeks and shook Harry's hand. "Loads of people I want you to meet," he said, pulling Dionne by her hand. Harry trailed along behind as Dionne was propelled towards a group of people on the far side of the yacht. James introduced them both to a group of people who were clearly in the finance business. As they all talked shop, Harry stood next to Dionne getting increasingly bored, and trying hard not to let it show.

A slim brunette sidled up beside him, and thrust her hand out. "Hello, I'm Christina, James' girlfriend, are you Harry Cooper?" She asked, smiling, and pulling him away from the group.

"Pleased to meet you, yes I'm Harry," he replied, shaking her hand.

"Bloody boring aren't they? I can't understand a word they're on about," she whispered, nodding at the group of men hanging onto Dionne's every word.

"Not many people can," agreed Harry.

"Who's the woman?" Christina asked, pointing at Dionne.

"My girlfriend, Dionne, she's a financier too." Harry's heart swelled with pride saying those words.

"James can't take his eyes off her, that means he'll be a prick to you. Guess it means my days are numbered," she grinned. "Not that I care, as long as I get a pay off. He's a total dickhead on occasion, and a nasty bastard the rest of the time."

Harry gaped at her. "Why are you with him if you feel like that?" He asked.

"Cos he's rich, he's got a yacht, and it's better than working for a living," she said, jutting out her chin. An idea was forming in her mind of moving on to the handsome film star, and was appealing more and more. "Your girlfriend suits him far better than I do," she said, feigning despondency. She stared pointedly at the sight of James holding Dionne's elbow as they chatted to the group. "Don't they just make the perfect power couple?"

Looking over, Harry's stomach dropped. He could see exactly what she meant. Two charismatic, powerful people who looked totally at ease together. At that moment, he didn't feel like 'The' Harry Cooper, film star. He felt like the hick cousin, the poor relation. A lifetime of insecurities reared their ugly heads and made him want to cling to Dionne. He didn't, instead he just stood there, sick with jealousy, and inadequacy, and trying not to let it show.

James whispered in Dionne's ear, "looks like the pretty people are getting along well."

Dionne turned to see Harry and Christina chatting, although she couldn't hear what they were saying. She caught his eye, and smiled.

"Wouldn't those two breed the most beautiful babies?" James sneered, glancing over to Christina.

"Jealous?" Inquired Dionne.

"Hell no, he's welcome to her. Pretty girl but not much going on upstairs if you know what I mean," he winked. "Or do you prefer yours pretty but dim?" James' eyes burned into her as he asked the question.

"I like gentlemen, not players," replied Dionne, "and if I'd wanted a rich player, I would have gone out with Darren Karrett when he asked me."

"That little pauper? Oh come on Di, you can do better than that. You need an equal, not a wannabe or a pretty boy. It's not fair to play them along and dump em when you get bored looking at them. You told me that once I recall."

Dionne briefly pondered his words before dismissing them with a "It's not like that with Harry, he's not in any way dim, and I can't see me getting bored. Besides after twenty years with anyone it gets a bit samey, you don't dump them for it, you just evolve with them. You should try it sometime James."

"I'd try it with the right woman Dionne," said James, staring at her cleavage.

Dionne excused herself and went to stake her claim on Harry by wrapped her arm through his and kissing his cheek.

"Shall we check out the rest of the boat?" She said, mainly to get him away from Christina, who had a predatory look in her eyes.

"Thank you for rescuing me," said Harry, kissing her on the cheek. "That Christina was a bit of a piece of work. She's only with him for his money you know."

Dionne laughed. "I think he's quite happy with that arrangement.

He's only with her for one thing too, so they make a perfect couple."

For the remainder of the party, they stuck together, chatting to other couples. Harry was frequently recognised, and happily posed for pictures with various starstruck women. Dionne observed him closely, watching how he donned a mask-like expression for photos, always tilting his face slightly to the left.

By the time they left, all thoughts of jealousy had gone, and Harry had regained his composure.

Their last few days in Barbados were spent lounging around the pool, making love, and generally relaxing. Harry discovered it was pointless to try and play cards or chess with Dionne, and she discovered it wasn't possible to beat him at tennis.

They returned to London the second week of December, arriving late morning at London City airport. Harry planned to spend the afternoon at home, catching up with his post and other errands, while Dionne caught up with her work. They arranged to meet for dinner at seven at Dionne's house afterwards, as they both decided neither wanted to sleep alone. So Harry jumped in a taxi at the airport, and made his way to South Kensington.

CHAPTER 8

Hollie Cranwell was resourceful. She had found Harry's home address on the electoral register, and discovered he was in Barbados via twitter. She had prepared what she needed very carefully, purchasing some items over the internet, and sat outside his house quietly watching from her car.

At midday, she watched a small Phillipino woman let herself in using a key. Shortly afterwards, there was an Ocado delivery. *'He must be coming home today'* she thought. Hollie knocked on the door a few minutes later.

"Hello, I'm Hollie, Mr Cooper asked me to measure up for new curtains, he said you would be here to let me in," she said with a bright smile. The maid stood aside and allowed her in, not really able to understand what the smiling lady had said as her English was very limited.

Hollie walked through into the kitchen and placed her holdall on the island, unzipped it and drew out a tape measure. The maid, satisfied, left to carry on her hoovering. Twenty minutes later, she returned to the kitchen, puzzled when she couldn't see the woman. From behind the door, Hollie grabbed her, and held a cloth over her face. Within seconds the maid slumped to the floor. Hollie grabbed a roll of duct tape from her holdall, and bound and gagged the maid securely. She dragged the maid out of sight of the front door, and sat and waited.

Hollie jumped slightly when she heard a key turning in the front door. She quickly impregnated the cloth again, and hid behind the kitchen door, her heart beating a frantic pace.

Harry had no chance as he walked into the kitchen. He barely even registered the hand holding something over his face before he slumped to the floor. She bound his hands and feet with the tape, leaving his beautiful mouth uncovered. It took her a while to drag him into the middle of the kitchen floor as he was so heavy. She found a pair of scissors in her holdall, and proceeded to carefully cut his clothes off. When he was naked, she pulled a chair over to sit and wait for him to wake up, and to admire his unclothed body.

She gazed wistfully at his smooth, tanned skin, and lightly ran her fingers over his chest hair. She stared at his penis, wondering how it would have felt inside her. She took it in her hand. Even flaccid it felt thick and heavy. *'Such a shame to have to do this, but he can't keep cheating on me and making me jealous. He has to learn that I love him like no other, I am his, and he is mine.'*

As Harry began to come to, his mind couldn't fathom why his arms wouldn't move, and why he felt so cold. He slipped in and out of consciousness for a few hours until his kitchen began to come into focus. He tried to move, and found he couldn't. He also couldn't work out why he was naked. The overhead lights were harsh and were blinding him, so he couldn't see what was going on. Eventually his eyes adjusted, the fog in his mind cleared, and he was able to make out a woman sitting on a chair in front of him.

"Hello Harry. I doubt if you remember me. I'm Hollie, your biggest fan. We met in that cafe in Chelsea when you cheated on me with that bitch." She sneered in a way that made Harry's scalp prickle.

"What on earth are you doing? This is my house, how did you get in?" He demanded.   She nodded towards the island. He followed her gaze, and saw the maid bound and gagged, her eyes terrified.

"What do you want?" He asked the deranged woman.

She laughed, "I want you to realise that I exist, that I love you far more than anyone else ever could. I want you to stop cheating on me. I would have even let you stick that in me if you'd have asked," she said, gesturing to his penis.

"This is not the right way to go about it. Are you aware of kidnap laws?" Demanded Harry, getting angrier and angrier.

"Oh yes, but you see, you were nasty when we met, and then you cheated. Your penis belongs to me, not her, so I'm going to take it."

Harry went cold, *no, this cannot be happening, keep her talking, charm her, anything, fuck.*

"What's your name?" He asked her, trying to keep his voice even.

"Hollie, see, you didn't even remember it, I told you it before. I run your Facebook page."

"Thank you for that Hollie, it's probably due to you that I got the last few roles, they saw how many fans I had you see." Harry was grasping at anything at this point.

Meanwhile, Dionne looked at the clock, puzzled. It was seven o'clock. Harry had never been late for anything in his life. She tried his phone, and it went straight to voicemail. A sense of unease crept over her. She called Craig and asked him to go check on Harry, as she was sure there was something wrong. Craig decided to whizz over on his motorbike as it would be faster. He grabbed Harry's keys and set off.

Harry was trying to keep her talking. He could see the kitchen clock from his position on the floor. The hands had crept round to 7.15. He prayed that Dionne would notice him missing. Hollie broke his train of thought by pulling a pair of bolt cutters from her holdall.

"I'm going to remove your penis with this. That way you won't be able to cheat anymore, and I won't have to get jealous," she said calmly, as if it was a perfectly normal thing to say.

'No no anything but this, what about Dionne? I can't lose her. No anything but this, please God'. Prayed Harry.

"Please Hollie, please don't do this. I could bleed to death. Please, I'll give you anything, I'm begging you not to do this." Harry pleaded, his eyes betraying his terror.

"Stop it, or I'll drug you again, and do it while you're asleep." Hollie said quietly.

Craig could see lights on in Harry's kitchen, so walked round the side to have a look. The moment he saw what was going on through the window, he slipped back round to the front, coded for backup and silently turned his spare key in the door.

As Hollie drew the bolt cutters open, she heard a click behind her.

A male voice said "drop the bolt cutters, or I will blow your head off." Craig was standing behind her holding a gun to her head. Hollie dropped the heavy cutters onto Harry's feet, breaking one of his toes. She raised her hands, and began to cry.

'This isn't how it's meant to pan out, oh my god, what's gonna happen?' Thought Hollie.

"Have you called the police?" Harry asked Craig, he just nodded. *'Thank fuck'* thought Harry.

Craig stood silently until both the police, and other members of the security crew arrived. Hollie was handcuffed, arrested and taken away quickly. Craig freed Harry and his maid, and accompanied them both to hospital. The other security men stayed with the police and supervised the collection of evidence before ensuring Harry's house was properly locked up again.

During the journey to the hospital, Harry phoned Dionne from Craig's mobile. He knew he wasn't making much sense as the adrenaline was making him shake and gabble. He still felt odd from the chloroform, and couldn't seem to warm up. He just about remembered Craig asking him if he was alright before he passed out.

Dionne and Lynne made their way to St Johns Wood, arriving at the Wellington hospital shortly after Harry. They were shown to a waiting room where they could sit while the doctors checked out both Harry and his maid. Craig came and found them, and told them what had happened, while Dionne sat with her hand over her mouth, the full horror of what could have been, running through her mind.

Lynne gave Ralph a call, figuring he would need to deal with the press. Dionne reached for her phone as well, and called her lawyer. She described the events of the evening, gave the woman's name and the police station she was being held, and parted with,

"Throw everything you got at her, section her, anything, just make sure she is never free to go near Harry again." Dionne jabbed angrily at the phone to end the call.

Lynne rubbed her friend's arm. "Hey, he's ok, you saved him."

"I just feel so fucking angry Lynne. How dare she threaten him like that. How could she have wanted to do that to him. I want to kill her with my own bare hands, I'm so angry. The sick little bitch needs to rot in a hellhole."

Dionne paced around the waiting room, her anger taking hold of her. "His body is completely perfect, how could anyone want to ruin it?"

"I think it's pretty clear she's not all the ticket Di, the girl was totally loopylou to even think of what she did, let alone carry it out. Let's just be thankful he's still in one piece."

A doctor came into the waiting room, "Dionne?" He asked. Dionne stood back up.

"Yes, how's Harry?" She demanded.

"He's fine, shocked and a bit disorientated, but we strapped up his toe, and there appears to be no lasting damage. He's asking to see you, so if you'd like to follow me." The doctor gestured to the door.

Harry was dozing when Dionne and Lynne appeared. They sat each side of his bed, and Dionne grasped his hand, which woke him up.

"Di, I thought for a while back there that I'd never see you again, or if I survived, I'd lose you," he said quietly.

115

"Oh baby, I'm so sorry this happened to you. It must have been terrifying. I love every bit of you though, not just your dick, just so you know," replied Dionne, eliciting a weak smile from Harry.

Lynne noticed that Harry's other hand was under the covers. "Is the old chap ok after his fright?" She asked.

"He's practically hiding still, but no, she didn't actually hurt it. Craig got there just in time. Your security really are very good Di," he said, keeping his hand where it was.

Dionne wrapped her arms around his shoulders and hugged him tight. Her tears finally began to fall.

"Hey baby, don't cry, I'm fine. Your security saved me yet again. Hey, come on now." He released his hand to wrap around Dionne and pull her in to a tight hug. She sobbed loudly into his neck while he stroked her back. Eventually she stopped crying and managed a weak smile.

Lynne reached over to rub both their hands. "See he's fine," she said.

The door opened and Ralph walked in. After all the hello's, Harry recounted the story again, while Ralph went pale.

"Fuck, what a horror story. Well I'll deal with all the press for you. There are reporters camped outside the hospital waiting for the low down, and wanting to find out if The Harry Cooper is alive and well," said Ralph kindly.

Dionne gave him her lawyer's number so he could clarify exactly what he could tell the press. Ralph went off to deal with the lawyer and the reporters, leaving Lynne and Dionne.

Lynne stood up. "I'm going to check on your maid, just in case she doesn't have family. Be back in a bit, do you want anything?" she asked.

They both shook their heads, grateful to be alone for a while. Dionne leaned over to kiss Harry, revelling in the feel of her sensual, beautiful

116

man.

He stroked her face. "I love you, and thank you for saving me....again."

"I love you too, and it's your obsession with punctuality that saved you. I knew at four minutes to seven that something was wrong."

The doctor entered the room. He checked Harry's eyes, toe, and blood pressure, and declared him fit to go home.

"How's Fenita?" Asked Harry, concerned about the little Philippino maid and her lack of English.

"She's fine, shocked, same as you really. We have a nurse who speaks her language which helped enormously. Her husband is on his way to collect her. Can I arrange transport home for her on your bill sir?" The doctor was very matter of fact.

"Yes of course, and I'll cover her bill here completely," said Dionne.

"You don't have to do that Di, I'll pay for it," said Harry.

"Erm, you were brought here naked. Where exactly are you stashing your wallet?" Giggled Dionne.

"Oh shit. How on earth am I gonna leave?" Said Harry, alarmed.

"My security have your keys, and are on their way over with some clothes. They're probably in the waiting room by now," she smiled. Just then, Lynne returned holding a small pile of clothing, and a jacket. She left the room, and paid the bill at the front desk while Harry got dressed, letting Dionne check out the fact that he really was still intact.

They were taken to an underground garage where Dionne's car was waiting for them. Joe whisked them through the throngs of reporters waiting outside, and went straight back to Dionne's house.

When the gates closed behind them, Harry finally began to feel safe again. He decided he was starving hungry, desperate for a coffee, and his toe was starting to throb.

They helped him in, and sat him down in the drawing room. Dionne put the news on to see if the story was being covered (it was), and Connor wheeled a trolley of food and drinks in, leaving it near Harry so he didn't have to move to reach it. Lynne pulled a footstool over to place under Harry's injured foot.

"It's quite good being poorly round your house Di, I'm gonna park myself here next time I have man flu," grinned Harry, enjoying the spoiling he was getting.

"Well, you've had a rotten day, it's the least we can do," chirped Lynne, plonking herself down on the sofa. Dionne handed her a coffee before pouring another one for herself and refilling Harry's cup.

"Is the chloroform out of your system now?" Dionne asked.

"I think so, I don't feel woozy anymore. My toe hurts though," he replied.

"The hospital gave me a cage to keep the bedclothes off it, Connor's putting it in our room," said Dionne, determined that Harry wasn't going home again.

That night in bed, for the first time, they didn't make love. Dionne was worried about hurting his foot, and Harry was just enjoying feeling safe and cared for. They snuggled up and fell asleep, both exhausted.

At 3am, Dionne was woken by a scream. Harry was flailing, screaming at his imaginary assailant to get off. Dionne tried to gently wake him, to no avail, and ended up shaking him harder to bring him back from wherever his mind was taking him. He came to with a start, drenched in sweat, his heart racing with fear. He slipped a hand down to check his dick, and then buried his face in her neck and cried. She rubbed his back soothingly, and held him until his crying stopped, his breathing evened out, and he went back to sleep.

The next day they both woke late, with neither of them feeling the need to jump out of bed immediately, they rang down for breakfast in bed. Dionne helped Harry shower with his injured foot sticking out of the shower door to keep it dry. She washed his hair, cleansed his face, and soaped him all over. She was delighted when he finally had an erection, and gently, but enthusiastically sucked him to orgasm in the shower.

He was relieved it still worked. It had been on his mind that his previous sexual issues, coupled with the castration attempt would cause his poor dick to hide from the world forever. His anxiety had increased when he discovered that he hadn't had a morning erection. Thankfully the sight of Dionne all naked and soapy in the shower had it springing back to life. They celebrated with another orgasm each, both being exceptionally gentle.

The press went nuts, much to Harry's embarrassment. He hated the thought of the whole world knowing he was found naked on his kitchen floor, and although Ralph had tried to contain things, Fenita had described how he had begged his attacker for mercy. After Fenita had told 'The Sun' how Harry's penis had shrivelled in fear, and resembled a small mushroom, Dionne put her foot down, and instructed her lawyer to slap a gagging order on her. Then she personally phoned the Home Secretary and asked him to deport the little bitch if at all possible.

She also insisted on 24 hour security for Harry. Craig sourced a team to provide close protection whenever Harry went out. After a few days, the subject of his return home had to be addressed. Harry brought up the issue after dinner.

"Di, you will tell me if I've overstayed my welcome won't you," he mumbled, not looking at her. She regarded him intently.

"Of course I would. I like having you here, and I'm scared of you going home."

"But I don't live here Di, I have to go home sometime."

"Do you want to?" She enquired. Harry pondered the question. In truth he didn't particularly want to return to the scene of his nightmare, but he did miss the normality of it, and the privacy he had there. Living at Dionne's was like being in a gilded goldfish bowl, with the staff watching every move. He suddenly had a craving for egg and chips, and some crap telly.

When Harry didn't answer, she sighed." What is it?".

He scrubbed at his face "I need some normality Di. I need crap telly, some junk food, to sit around in just my pants, you know, that kind of thing. I don't actually want to go home as such, but I do need a bit of a break from all this," he said, waving his hand across the beautifully dressed table of food laid out in front of them.

"Fine," said Dionne, rising up from the table. "I'll see you tomorrow maybe," and with that, left the room and strode down the corridor to her office.

Harry was at a bit of a loss as to what to do. He regretted bringing up the matter of his going home, as it had clearly upset her. He debated following her into her office, but decided he ought to go home as he'd caused this issue in the first place. He wandered through the kitchen to find his bodyguard and head back to Pondbury Gardens.

The house was freezing when he walked in. He switched the heating on, and showed the bodyguard to his guest room. Once the security guard was out of the way, Harry flicked on the large telly in his lounge. He made himself a coffee, noticing the food in the fridge was mostly out of date, and grabbed a bag of peanuts before flopping on the sofa to watch a trashy police show.

Unable to settle, he wondered what Dionne was doing. Determined not to go running back to her, he pulled out his Xbox and started playing 'call of duty'. Somehow he couldn't get into it, so that too was abandoned. He checked his phone. She hadn't called. He checked his emails, scrolling through the advertising spam and studio memos, nothing from her. 'Damn' he thought.

Meanwhile, Dionne was sulking in her office. She realised that Harry had needed some space, and in truth, so did she, but it had been a bit sudden, and felt like a rejection. She decided to leave him be for the night, and catch up on some work.

The deal with Douggie had concluded while she had been in Barbados, which had made her extremely cash rich. She sat and thought about her plan to sell off assets, which at that moment felt a bit pointless, as she already had enough cash for fifty lifetimes. To have cash sitting doing nothing went against the grain, normally it would be reinvested quickly to gain either assets which would appreciate in value, or shares which would generate more cash. It took monumental self discipline for her to just do nothing.

When she had finished her emails, she chose a book from her library and went upstairs. She ran a deep bath, carefully adding her favourite oil, and sank in, enjoying the solitude. *'I've missed this'*. She resolved to pull back from Harry a little, and make sure she had more alone time again.

She switched on her tv as she got into bed, finding a decent documentary on the fall of the Roman Empire to watch, she sank back into the pillows, and relaxed.

By midnight, Harry was seriously regretting going home. His house felt lonely, empty, and a bit scary. He doubted whether he'd be able to sleep, even with the security man keeping watch. He debated calling Dionne, wrestling with the decision. If he did call, he would seem needy and weak. If he didn't call, she might think he didn't want her. He picked up his iPhone, and scrolled down to her number.

'Fuck it, I'll be needy and weak then' he thought as he dialled.

"Hi"

 "Hi"

"What are you doing?" He asked her, wincing at how dopey he sounded.

 "Sleeping"

"Oh, sorry, did I wake you?" He winced again.

"Yes, I just told you I was sleeping. It's midnight. What do you want Harry?"

"I miss you. Are you missing me?"

Dionne sighed. "I'm enjoying a bit of solitude if I'm truthful."

"Oh." Dionne could hear the disappointment in his voice.

"I wish I hadn't come back here. I don't know what I was thinking," he said despondently.

"Just go to sleep Harry, I'll see you tomorrow," she said before cutting the call, not giving him the chance to reply. She switched her phone to silent, and turned off the lights before drifting off.

She woke up when the bed dipped, a certain large male body trying to sneak in without waking her. She smiled in the darkness when a large muscular arm gently wrapped around her, and a perfectly sculptured mouth let out a little sigh of contentment.

The following evening, Dionne organised a takeaway curry to be delivered. She gave the waiting and kitchen staff the evening off, and (gritting her teeth somewhat) sat through 'Eastenders' and 'A question of sport' while Harry sat in his boxers enjoying himself.

The following day, he moved in. He decided to put his house up for rent rather than sell it, so the movers only had to deal with his personal things. His clothes were hung neatly in the spare dressing room by Connor, who ensured that everything was perfectly pressed. Even the old, over washed superman pyjamas were beautifully ironed, and folded innocently in a drawer.

CHAPTER 9

Thoughts turned to Christmas. It was decided that the four of them would spend the holiday in the Cotswolds. Lynne wanted some quality time with Dan, as he had been busy preparing for his next film, which had required a lot of costume fittings, plus hours in the gym to bulk up his physique. Their burgeoning relationship was progressing well. Dan had an easy charm which had punched through Lynne's considerable defences. She loved his slightly offbeat personality, and he loved her wicked sense of humour. The two of them were spending increasing amounts of time together, schedules permitting, and slowly but surely falling for each other.

Dionne pulled some strings to get access to both Harrods and Harvey Nichols after hours. It was mostly Harry and Lynne who took advantage of it, but Dionne joined Harry for a shopping trip one evening to look for gifts for Lynne. Harry was a little surprised when Dionne pulled out a list of potential gifts she had drawn up. She explained that through the year she noted down whenever Lynne mentioned that she liked, or wanted something. A few of the items were decidedly mundane, which he thought was quite comical. He also paid close attention to anything Dionne said was nice as they wandered through the store.

He gulped at bit at the amount Dionne spent. She bought Lynne a handbag that was *ten thousand quid*, as well as jewellery, cosmetic stuff, and an iPad with real diamonds around the edge. He trailed along as she bought presents for Dan that included a new gaming system, and a pair of platinum cuff links. He mused that shopping with her resembled a trolley dash, as she picked out gifts quickly, didn't look at the price, and just sent them off to be gift wrapped by the staff who were so overly attentive it was hilarious.

By the time they had finished, Dionne paid her bill which was over four hundred thousand pounds, and arranged for the gifts to be delivered to Upper Slaughter the following day.

Lynne had guided him with his gifts, which he was pleased with. He had also donned a hat and dark glasses, and made a foray over to the sex shops of Soho, to purchase some gifts of a more personal nature, smuggling them into Lynne's house for her to wrap.

She had laughed her head off at some of the items, knowing Dionne would love them, plus she enjoyed teasing Harry, as he was so repressed, it was almost funny.

She paused at a book of tantric sex that Harry had purchased, flicking through it. "This looks interesting, I might borrow it when Di's read it."

"Don't you dare tell her I showed you this stuff. She would be terribly embarrassed," said Harry looking horrified.

"Who do you think bought the anal vibrator, and the vibrating cock ring that you're so fond of?" Lynne replied, watching, amused, as Harry turned puce.

"Oh sweet Jesus, is there anything you don't know?" He muttered, unable to look at her.

She laughed. "Nope, and it's lucky I'm unshockable. Di tells me everything. I tell her everything too, so it's even, and Dan is far kinkier than you."

Harry desperately wanted to ask her to elaborate, but held back, not wanting to embarrass her. He resolved to ask Dionne later.

The four of them flew down to the Cotswolds on Christmas Eve, just getting there before the bad weather crept in. The house looked like a fairy tale mansion, artful arrangements of tiny white lights were draped over the facade, and the trees lining the drive were all twinkling prettily.

With fat flakes of snow falling around them, the whole scene looked magical.

The foyer was dressed in traditional decorations made of holly and other greenery, and was dominated by a huge tree hung exclusively with gold baubles. With an enormous fire blazing in the fireplace, the total effect was stunning, and smelt wonderful. Harry felt suddenly homesick for something which he couldn't define, either a feeling or a memory from long ago.

They all shed their coats and made their way to the drawing room, where some mulled wine and hot mince pies were waiting.

The London staff had been shipped down for the holiday to assist Janice and Terry. The task of organising the decorations and festivities fell on Lynne as usual, which she loved. She enjoyed sourcing special food, rare wines, and dealing with the specialist florists who had created the magical displays.

Not for the first time, Dionne felt a pang of sadness that her friend had never had a family. Lynne would have loved children, and would have been a wonderful mother. Dionne allowed herself to daydream for a moment about a couple of little ones racing around the large house on Christmas morning, little feet pedalling new trikes along the grand gallery. The thought made her smile wistfully. She resolved that if Harry and her lasted, they would invite his brothers and their families to future Christmases.

She was snapped out of her maudlin reverie by Dan yelling at Harry to look under the tree. The sight of two beautiful, urbane men sitting cross legged beside the tree rummaging through parcels, shaking them excitedly, made the two women laugh out loud.

After dinner, they watched telly together, which was film featuring talking cats. Harry discovered that Dionne loved any film with talking animals, which he found quite endearing. She explained that as a child, her father had told her that at midnight, on Christmas Eve, the animals spoke. As she had grown up with cats, she was about twelve before she stopped believing they had conversations with her father every

Christmas.

They all sat discussing their childhood Christmases. It turned out Dan had a vast, extended family, and his Christmases were rowdy, loud affairs, involving drunken Aunties and boisterous cousins. Dionne asked Harry about his.

"Well, up until Mum died, they were fun. I remember her cooking, and having our presents in pillowcases on Christmas morning, and my brothers and I having all the chocolates off the tree before Christmas Eve. After Mum died, we didn't have Christmas. Dad didn't bother, and we had no other family. This is the first time I really celebrated it since I was six. My two older brothers are both married, so their wives organise them, and my younger two, well I'm not too sure what they do."

"Your first Christmas in 24 years?" Asked Dionne incredulously.

"Yup," replied Harry. "I generally spent Christmas Day either at home, on my own, or if I was filming, in a hotel. It's no biggie, I just didn't bother with it. I like all this though," he said, sweeping his hand towards the decorations and presents.

As usual, Lynne broke the melancholy. "Well in which case, we need to make sure you have fun then Harry. Who's up for a game of twister?"

They opened a bottle of champagne, and spread the game out on the floor. Soon they were helpless with laughter after Dionne had been squashed beneath Lynne and Harry, and in her best schoolmarm voice asked Lynne to remove her face from Harry's crotch, eliciting a muffled "I can't," from Lynne.

Christmas morning brought a blanket of fresh snow, giving the countryside a picture perfect quality. Dionne came to slowly, peeling her eyes open after too much champagne the night before. She started when she realised Harry was wide awake and staring at her. He grinned broadly, before kissing her quickly, and scooting down the bed to retrieve a novelty stocking.

"Merry Christmas, I've been waiting ages for you to wake up," he said, almost bouncing with excitement.

"Ok ok, just give me a minute to wake up. Call down for coffee would you? Let me find your stocking," said Dionne, thinking the whole 'staring at her sleeping' thing was a bit creepy. She retrieved his stocking from under the bed, and plopped it into his lap, watching as he almost clapped his hands in glee, stopping himself at the last moment.

They took turns opening their presents. Dionne received beautiful underwear, perfume, cashmere gloves, and other assorted goodies. Harry was wide eyed at his gifts, platinum cufflinks, a vertu iPhone with a sapphire screen, an iPad mini, which wasn't even out yet, and Christmas socks.

"How on earth did you get hold of this?" He asked, holding up the iPad.

"Pulled some strings, I'm a big old shareholder," she giggled.

'Of course she is' he thought.

"Well I think I ought to say thank you properly," he breathed, sliding his body over hers. Desire coursed through her at the feel of his silky skin, her body heating under his touch. Sliding his lips down her neck, his mouth found her nipple, sucking on it, he slid his hand down between her legs. "Oh you are so ready," he breathed.

She caressed his cheek, lifting him up from her nipple. "Our coffee will be here in a minute. Let's not frighten the staff." She kissed him as he sighed and flopped onto his back. A few moments later there was a knock on the door. She slipped on her robe, and let Connor in with their coffees.

"Merry Christmas ma'am, sir," he said stiffly before leaving. Dionne locked the door behind him.

"Now where were we?" She purred, letting the robe slide off her shoulders.

The four of them had a champagne breakfast before settling into the games room. The two men played with their new ipads, while Dionne and Lynne chatted about their presents. Dan had bought Lynne a necklace, a DVD of advanced yoga, and some sexy underwear.

They had a huge lunch served in the formal dining room, Lynne giving a bit of a running commentary on the provenance of the exquisite food and drinks that they were served. After two helpings of Fortnum and Mason Christmas pudding, and a final glass of Beaume de Venise, Harry undid his trouser button, and sat back with a contented sigh.

"I have never seen a person eat so much in one sitting," observed Dionne.

"Mans gotta eat. That was gorgeous by the way," said Harry, "but I need to sit in a soft chair now," he added.

They all slumped into the sofas in the drawing room, switching on the telly for the queens speech. Dan distributed the pile of presents and they each took it in turns to open. Dionne was astonished that Harry had got her a book of erotic stories (which he promised to read to her in his sultry baritone), as well as various items from an upmarket adult shop, which made her blush.

Lynne laughed when she opened a gift box containing a sexy maids outfit from Dan, calling him 'a kinky bugger'. Dan thought it even funnier when he opened an elaborately wrapped box containing a bumper selection of male sex toys.

Harry began to sweat slightly, wondering what Dionne had got him, apart from the leather jacket, sweaters and shirts he had already opened. Dionne opened the book of tantric sex, and seemed pleased, only one more each to open.

"Open your last one Di," said Harry, anxious. She pulled on the paper to reveal a small Tiffany box. Opening it, she pulled out a platinum heart, studded with rubies and diamonds, on a platinum chain. It was beautiful, simple, and loving. Her eyes filled up.

"It's beautiful, thank you so much," she whispered, pulling Harry into an embrace. "Open yours," she urged. Harry tore at the paper to reveal a small box. Inside was a watch. Dionne had bought him a Patek Phillipe platinum tourbillon 5002. It was a watch that Harry had promised he would treat himself to one day. He was almost speechless.

"I wanted one of these," was all he managed to blurt out. He pulled Dionne into a hug, not trusting himself to say any more.

Dionne held her hair up so that Harry could put the necklace on her, and he watched as she stroked it reverently. He put on his new watch, and sat reading the instructions.

That afternoon, Lynne and Dan went for a walk through the grounds while Dionne read the book on tantric sex. Harry snored slightly as he dozed off watching a bond film, prompting an indulgent smile from Dionne.

That night, Dionne decided to try out the first few tantric exercises with Harry, who was happy to oblige. They sat in the centre of the large bed, Harry sitting upright, with Dionne facing him, straddled, and impaled on his erection. She had explained that the idea was to make it last as long as possible by building intimacy without moving.

"Right, ok, I'll give it a shot," he said, unconvinced.

They gazed into each other's eyes, their breath merging, and slowly caressed each other. Harry loved the feel of her skin, sliding his hands over her lean back, feeling the curve of her waist. He tried to resist the temptation to move, to get some friction. His sense of anticipation reached higher and higher peaks. He stared into her bright blue eyes, looking for clues as to how she was feeling, what she was feeling. He felt totally connected with her, as if they were one person.

Eventually she spoke. "Darling I really have to move, I have cramp in my thighs."

"Let me lay you down then. I can stay still in you that way. I'm liking this," he replied, not wanting to stop, but feeling he had to make her comfortable. Staying inside her, he lifted her slightly, and laid her on her back, his body cradled in hers. He rested his weight on his elbows, and continued to remain still, the slight movement increasing his arousal intensely.

He shifted his weight to balance on one elbow so he could caress her breast, sending synapses of pleasure coursing through her. Dionne felt the waves of arousal overcoming her, encompassing her entire body. Unable to remain still any longer, she tilted her hips slightly, trying to find the friction she craved so much.

Harry exploded first, the orgasm pumping out of him with such intensity that Dionne felt it inside. Seeing him lose control tipped her over the edge, her climax pulsing in waves of pleasure through her entire body, lasting much longer than normal. Harry felt her rippling around him, squeezing him intimately. He watched as her skin bloomed pink across her chest, before gently kissing her reddened lips.

"What did you think?" She enquired.

"Liked it. Was a bit of a struggle to stay still though, halfway through I just wanted to start pounding. What about you? You came for a long time."

"Hmm, it was a different kind of orgasm. It was good, but I think I prefer our more explosive sex. Plus we were at it for an hour and a half, and you missed that program you wanted to see," she smirked.

"In which case we might as well test out more vigorous techniques, so we can compare," winked Harry, reaching into the bedside cabinet for his cock ring and her vibrator.

Another hour later, they lay catching their breath, letting their bodies cool down. Harry spoke first.

"Lynne told me that Dan is far kinkier than me, what does she mean by that?"

Dionne laughed. "He likes anal, and doing it in public, so yeah, I'd say he was kinkier than you."

"He likes doing Lynne up the bum? Wonder why he likes that?" Harry mused, never once having had the desire to try it.

"No silly, he likes her to do it to him," sniggered Dionne, amused at Harry's look of horror.

"No way," he breathed, "how?"

"Strap-on."

Harry winced. "In public too? Wow, he is pervy."

"That's what they get off on. Lynne likes it too you know, I think those two are kindred spirits. I've had to pay coppers off on more than one occasion when Lynne's been caught shagging in public," said Dionne, shrugging at Harry's astonishment.

"No way," he exclaimed, horrified. "I had no idea Dan was into all that. Do you think he's gay?"

"No, just a bit of a perv," laughed Dionne. "Lynne used to be a member of a sex club at one time." She observed Harry closely to see his reaction.

"Wow, never would have thought of her being like that," said Harry, not missing a beat.

'Hmm, no reaction to the mention of a sex club, maybe Adam was wrong' she thought as she dozed off.

CHAPTER 10

They returned to London just after new year. Harry had costume fittings and other pre- production jobs to take care of, so was pretty busy every day until he flew to LA the following week.

He was also tired of the constant security shadowing his every move. He wanted a visit to The Chamber before being stuck in LA for the next few months. Although he'd had more sex with Dionne than in the rest of his life put together, it wasn't the same thing as the deep need that was satisfied at the club. He made the decision to try and give his bodyguard the slip for a few hours, which proved extremely difficult.

Two days before he was due to fly, he was getting desperate. He had another costume meeting near Piccadilly, so booked The Nursery for afterwards. He insisted the bodyguard wait in the reception of the Universal offices, rather than trailing along behind.

Harry calmly and patiently completed his work at the studio offices before climbing out of a ground floor window and hailing a taxi to Belgrave Square. He checked that he hadn't been followed, and satisfied he was alone, rang the bell.

Meanwhile, unbeknown to Harry, all hell had broken loose. The moment it was discovered that he was missing, his guard had called Craig, who immediately put a trace on his mobile phone. Craig interrupted Dionne's work to inform her that Harry was unaccompanied and at an address in Belgrave Square, which made her heart sink.

She took the Bentley over there, not quite sure what she would do when she got there. They pulled up outside, and she got out. She spotted the tiny sign confirming it was indeed The Chamber. Wracked with indecision as to what to do, she was standing there just as Harry came out.

Any thoughts of relaxation deserted him as he came face to face with the woman he loved. His stomach dropped into his boots as he saw disappointment and anger flash across her eyes.

"Was I not enough for you?" She demanded, a hard edge to her voice which made Harry panic.

"It's not what you think, of course you're enough," he replied, desperately trying to think of an explanation or excuse.

"I think we should discuss this at home, not in the street," said Dionne flatly. She turned and got in the car, unable to look at him. He got in with her, and they sat in silence all the way back to the house, Dionne refusing to even look at him.

He followed as she strode straight into her office.

"So what were you doing there? Fucking someone, whipping or being whipped? Come on Harry I deserve an explanation." She spat the words out, clearly livid.

"How did you find out where I was?" Was all he could say.

"When you went missing, Craig got a lock on your mobile," replied Dionne," don't try and dodge the question."

Harry scrubbed at his face, knowing he couldn't tell her, unable to bear the thought of seeing her disgust, or worse, her pity.

"I can't tell you, please Di, I don't want to share this with you," he said sullenly.

"WHAT?" She exploded. "I catch you coming out of a fucking sex club, and you don't want to explain why, or what you were up to? How about my feelings? I have to wonder about you getting it elsewhere, giving me god knows what diseases, and wanting it with someone else.

How would you like it if I did that to you?"

Harry looked down at the floor. He had never seen Dionne truly angry before, and she was beyond livid right now. He cursed his own stupidity for going there, and for needing it.

"Tell me," she shouted, making him jump. He felt like a schoolboy in the principal's office.

"I can't."

"Can't or won't?"

"Won't," said Harry in a small voice.

Realising he wasn't going to tell her, she had to make a decision.

"Ok, fine, "she shouted, "have it your way, bear in mind that even the tightest lipped little dominatrix has her price, in the meantime, go to LA, and think about whether you miss me or not, because I will not be second best."

"You have never been second best," said Harry weakly, terrified that he was losing her.

"You have just had sex with another person. That makes me second best right now."

"I didn't have sex," said Harry.

"Did another man or woman see your dick?" Dionne demanded.

Harry paused.

"Don't you dare try and play word games with me, if someone else saw your dick, then you had sex. What was I, the rich, older woman you pityfucked while you kept your real sex life secret? That's what I believe right now." Dionne stormed out, leaving Harry at a total loss.

'This can't be happening. What the fuck do I do now? Shit shit think Harry think. You can't lose her' he thought.

He debated whether to stay at Dan's, or book a hotel to give her some space. Hearing the front door close, Harry looked out of the window to see the Bentley pulling out of the gates. *'Oh god, she's gone.'*

Harry climbed the stairs to their room in a daze. The thought of losing her was just too painful to contemplate. He would let her calm down and try to talk to her, remind her that he loved her. He tried to convince himself she would forgive him.

Meanwhile, Dionne was on her way to Upper Slaughter. Her anger was dissipating, replaced by a sadness of realisation that their relationship was over. She would stay away until he went to LA, and stay well away from him when he returned. She sat in the car and cried, the dam finally breaking.

Lynne was looking for Dionne, she walked into the bedroom, and found Harry packing.

"Didn't think you were leaving till Thursday," she said.

"Had a row with Di, so I'm going to change my flight to tomorrow. I don't know where she went, but I can't stay here," said Harry, looking panicked. Lynne sat down on the bed.

"I'll give her a call and see what's up with her. Calm down, you don't have to leave. What did you argue about anyway?"

"She caught me coming out of a club called The Chamber. Threw a wobbly at me, although I can't say as I blame her." Harry couldn't look at Lynne as he told her.

"What were you doing there?" Asked Lynne.

"I couldn't tell her, and I'm certainly not gonna tell you. It's not something I want to discuss," snapped Harry. Lynne regarded him intently, instantly understanding why Dionne had left.

"Well in which case, I take it you're not interested in carrying on your relationship with Di, because right now chances are she is doing a disappearing act until you're out of the way in LA, probably thinking you were just a gold digging player who fancied pulling the richest woman in the world for an ego trip."

"It's not like that and you know it. I'm not a player, and I'm most certainly no gold digger," he retorted, offended. *'Whoa, what the fuck is she on about with this richest woman in the world stuff?'*

"Oh I don't know, fucking about in a sex club while wearing a million quids worth of watch that she bought you....." She paused, "classy Harry."

"I'm in love with her, I don't want to lose her."

"Think it might be a bit late for that. I can't see Di being the type to share, or to sit at home happily while you play away. I know you saw the soft side of her, but believe me when I tell you she is not someone you fuck around with. She is tougher than pretty much any man on the planet."

"I'll grovel, she'll come around," stated Harry.

Lynne's eyes widened as she regarded the man her best friend was in love with.

"I cannot believe you are so naive, so totally clueless. You really don't have a scooby about her do you? She was married to one man for 18 years. She doesn't play around, and she won't forgive you for it either. Best I leave you to your packing." With that, Lynne left and returned to her own home to ring Dionne.

Harry sat on the bed and thought about their conversation, he had never loved before, let alone lost a lover. Women usually were the ones to cry and threaten when he hadn't wanted to see them again. Now he understood why. He wanted to follow Dionne and throw himself at her feet, begging forgiveness. Instead, he sat, paralysed, on her bed, wondering what the hell to do.

Dionne picked up on the first ring."Hi."

"Hi Di, Harry told me you had a row. Are you ok?" Asked Lynne, softly.

"Not really. Caught him coming out of that Chamber place, and he won't tell me what he was doing in there." She paused, "I feel such a fool. I didn't see it coming at all, thought he was happy, got that wrong didn't I?" She said sadly.

"I don't think you got anything wrong, you took a chance, and he fucked up. He won't even tell me what he was up to there. At the very least, you fucked a film star and rocked his world. Now let him go, and move on. Plenty of fish and all that," said Lynne, a touch too forcefully. She was angry with Harry too, and wanted him out of her friends life as quickly as possible, scared he would undo the good work she had done building Dionne's self confidence since John died.

"I'm going to stay at Upper Slaughter until he's gone. Can you organise storage for his things if he leaves anything behind please. I want no trace of him left in my house."

"Will do. Do you want me to come down?" Lynne asked.

"No, I want to be on my own for a few days."

Dionne's phone rang again as soon as she cut the call to Lynne. She could see it was Harry, so didn't answer.

Meanwhile, Lynne walked back over to Dionne's house. She found Harry sitting on the bed with a desolate look on his face.

"She won't talk to me. I know she has her phone, cos it was engaged for ages, and now she won't answer. How can we work this out if she won't talk to me?" He said, anguished.

"Harry, she asked me to put anything you don't take to LA into storage, she wants all traces of you gone before she comes back. I think it's safe to say its over." Lynne was matter of fact. Harry went pale, tears forming as he realised the enormity of what had just been said.

"Oh god, Lynne, please help me, I can't lose her, it took me my whole life to find her." The tears rolled down Harry's face as he spoke.

"You're an actor Harry, this is what you do for a living. I suggest you save it for your audiences, it won't work with me. You made the decision to slip your security and visit that place. Quite elaborate plans for just a quick shag, so my guess is you were up to more than that, and I know the type of thing catered for in those places. There's nothing that Di is gonna want to live with, so I suggest you get your pervy arse to LA, and forget about her." Lynne said with a forceful edge to her voice.

"I can't do that, I can't just forget her, I love her," he whispered. Lynne just turned and walked out of the room to brief the housekeeping and security teams.

The following day, Harry flew out to LA, unfortunately flying BA, as Dionne had cancelled the private plane she had organised for him. He didn't really care, just as he wasn't bothered that his security team had been withdrawn. He quite liked not having to put up with a bodyguard trailing along behind. He had been a bit mobbed at the airport, but Heathrow had plenty of security to whisk him away from the baying women who were thrusting camera phones in his face, and pestering for autographs.

He was a touch unnerved in the gents in first class, when a be-suited businessman had come on to him while he was having a pee. The man was slightly drunk, and very insistent, so Harry had to pee quickly, with the dirty bugger staring at his dick, and leg it back to the lounge before the man could get his hands on it.

Harry had forgotten what a pain in the arse fans could be. During the flight he was asked for autographs, photos, and was given six phone numbers. He tried to be the professional, and smile sweetly, but he was tired, depressed, and broken hearted.

'If I hadn't been such a tosser, I would have probably been on a private plane with Di right now, watching a film with my arms round her.'

A studio rep met him at LAX, pulling him through the waiting paps to a car. She handed him an itinerary, plus details of the apart-hotel he had been booked into.

"Sorry, it's not the best, but it was pretty short notice," she said apologetically. Harry glanced at it dismissively before muttering

"I'm sure it will be fine."

He pulled out his phone and tried Dionne again, cursing as it just rang and rang. He sent her a text to say he had landed safely, to add to the 500 or so unanswered texts he had sent already, his iPhone telling him that she had read them.

Compared to how he had been living, the apart-hotel was a third world country. The suite was tiny, barely the size of Dionne's bedroom, and the bathroom was more than slightly tired looking. Harry checked out the kitchen, surprised that nobody had thought to put any food in the fridge. He asked the studio rep to send a gopher out for some groceries, to be met with a hard stare.

"I'll ring round and see if there is an intern available with nothing to do, and no self esteem," she said sarcastically.

"Don't bother, I'll run down to the store on the corner and do it myself. Wouldn't want to put you out, given your important work," replied Harry, equally sarcastically.

'Asshole' she thought.

When she had gone, Harry stuck a hat and sunglasses on and went down to purchase some essential groceries, some coffee from a convenient Starbucks, and a pizza. Returning to the shabby suite, he flicked through the TV channels while he ate. He carefully unpacked and hung his clothes in the small closet, and took a shower in the grotty bathroom. The water came out of the shower head in a dribble, alternating between scalding and freezing. There were a couple of broken tiles, and some mould around the edge of the shower.

'Im having words with the studio tomorrow, there's no way I'm

140

staying here for four months' he thought.

He got into the lumpy bed, and lay staring at the ceiling for ages, contemplating all that he had lost. He knew he would have been comfortably ensconced in Dionne's Bel Air mansion, having staff catering for him, security guarding him, and an adorable blonde laying next to him to wrap himself around. His eyes welled up again.

'I miss her, how am I gonna get through this without her.'

Dionne was in her study. She had instructed the studio to house Harry in a grotty apartment, and deny him the usual assistance a star would normally get. She smiled to herself.

'Serve him right, that'll teach him to miss me' she thought.

She had read his increasingly desperate texts, and listened to the hundreds of voicemails he had left for her. He seemed to veer between grovelling sadly, and getting angry that she was ignoring him. She was waiting for a message that he was ready to tell her the truth about the sex club, before she would answer him, although some of the more desperate messages had tugged on her heart strings.

She missed him terribly, but was determined to push those feelings aside. Knowing that he had sought out kinky sex elsewhere was enough to make sure his heart rending voicemails didn't move her as much as they should.

Harry answered his phone. "Hi Dan, how's it going?"

"Great thanks, start filming next week, what about you?"

"Week after next. Final script run throughs next week. Where did the studio put you up? I'm in a bloody hellhole of an apartment."

Dan laughed, "I'm at Dionne's place in Bel Air, so no complaints from me, apart from the staff being a bit over attentive. I think they get bored here with nobody to look after, so I'm being lavished with fuss."

"She's still not speaking to me. Not sure quite what to do or say.

Wish I understood women a bit better," he said ruefully, envious of Dan's living arrangements.

"Do you want me to get the lowdown from Lynne? I can ask her later on when I call her. She's not coming out here till next week." Dan said kindly.

"Yeah, find out what you can. Is Dionne coming out next week as well then?" He asked.

"No. Think she was going to, but cancelled. Don't think she wants to run into you. Listen, why don't you come over tomorrow evening for a beer?"

Harry paused. "Do you think they would mind?"

"No, I already spoke to Lynne about it, it's fine, they don't expect me to cut you off. I'll organise beer and food. Bring your swimming gear as there's a great pool here."

"Great, see you tomorrow, text me the address." Harry said before ending the call.

Unable to sleep in his lumpy bed, Harry fired up his laptop. He checked his emails, seeing there were none from Dionne, he went into google. He typed in Dionne Devere, expecting it to come up blank as it had before they had got together. Instead, several pages of blogs and celeb gossip sites appeared. Clicking through the links, he saw picture after picture of the two of them together. Surprised, he clicked on images, seeing countless photos of the two of them together, most of which were taken without their knowledge.

He paused at the pictures of the two of them taken on the boat in Barbados. He remembered her blue dress, how elegant and summery she had looked, how proud he had been to show her off as his girlfriend. They had looked so happy and relaxed together, his arm was round her waist, holding them hip to hip.

He saved all the pictures to his laptop in case she had them scrubbed off the Internet, wondering why she had been happy to let these ones be on there.

'Maybe she doesn't know about them'

He googled Harry Cooper split, and saw that his predicament had already made the celebrity news sites. Thankfully the reason for the split hadn't been accurately reported, although it was being spitefully suggested that the age gap was the reason he had dumped her. Harry winced when he read the comments section, his fans writing that the split was good news as she was clearly too old for him, or she was covering up the fact he was gay, and it was time for him to come out of the closet.

He arrived at the Bel Air mansion at five to six the following day. Immediately turning green with envy at Dan's living arrangements. A butler served beers and meltingly soft steaks, accompanied by fries, salad and coleslaw. After eating, Dan showed him around.

Harry recognised Dionne's style in the house, the library shelves holding her type of books, and the office having the same banks of monitors as her office at home. Surveying the immaculate gardens, Harry was again overwhelmed with missing her. Dan was watching him closely.

"I spoke to Lynne last night," said Dan.

"Oh. Anything to report?" asked Harry.

"Yes, actually. She said that when one of your messages says you will tell Di the truth about that club, and what you were doing there, she'll listen."

Harry's stomach leapt.

'Willing to listen, not all lost then' he thought.

"Hmm. I'll give that some thought," he said, non committal.

"Christ Harry, do a bit more than that, you're missing her like mad, I can see that. According to Lynne, she's missing you, and it's not unreasonable for her to expect you to not fuck around. You are behaving like a bit of a prick over this, and I'm your mate, and on your side."

"I know Dan, but I can't tell her. I'm ashamed of it. Now can we leave it please?" Harry snapped, making Dan wonder what on earth Harry had been up to that was that bad.

Back in London, Dionne had thrown herself back into work. She was still holding off from buying, but was unravelling some holding companies, and surreptitiously selling off shares. Her cash pile was growing at a bit of an alarming rate, and it was taking every scrap of willpower she possessed not to start seeking out new investments, although a bit of a distraction would have been quite welcome. Her phone rang, seeing it wasn't Harry, she answered.

"James, how lovely to hear from you. How's everything?" She exclaimed.

"Great thanks Di. Sorry to read about you and the pretty chap, anyway, I have tickets for the Crystal Ball, would you like to accompany me?" Said James. "It's for a good cause," he added.

"What happened to Christina?"

"She wanted to go and be a Hollywood actress. I was bored with her, so set her up with some contacts, flew her to LA, and said goodbye nicely."

Dionne considered his invitation. Lynne would be away, so James' invite would be a nice diversion for an evening. He was a decent man, and although not quite up to Harry's standard, was pretty easy on the eye.

"That would be lovely James, thank you for asking. I'd be delighted," she said, smiling.

The next couple of weeks passed in a flurry of activity for Harry, with final script changes and costume alterations to do. He was interrupted on set by a studio bigwig one afternoon.

"Hi Harry, we need a bit of a favour. New starlet needs escorting to the Grammys tonight. We had Luke Evans lined up for her, but he's down with food poisoning, so you were suggested."

Harry sighed. He hated this side of the business. An evening babysitting some vacuous little wannabe was just what he didn't need. "Do I have to?"

"Yes. It's important for her new film. Wouldn't hurt for you to have some decent exposure as well." Was the answer.

He went back to the grotty apartment and changed into his tux. The car sent to pick him up was ten minutes late, which annoyed him. He jumped in to find Christina sitting there.

"Hi Harry! I'm so glad it's you tonight. I'm so nervous," she giggled.

'Oh great, just what I need' he thought.

"How nice to see you again Christina, just follow my lead, and we will get through this ok. Oh and please don't drink, I cannot deal with drunk women," he added.

'Twat' she thought, *'good looking one though'*

Harry sat back in his seat, feeling dreadful. He knew she was going to be all over him like a rash, and he hated prising starlet's grabby little hands off him after these 'fauxmance' appearances.

"Why aren't you happy about taking me to this?" Christina asked, jutting her chin out.

"Because I have better things to do than babysit you, and I hate the pretend romances the studio makes us do. I would actually rather stay at home plucking my nose hair than be here with you. Just so you know." Replied Harry petulantly.

"Maybe you shouldn't pretend. We could make this a real date, with a nice ending," purred Christina, looking flirtily over at him. He simply looked disgusted at her.

"Forget it, you have no chance," he spat.

A moment later, the limo doors were opened, and he took Christina's arm as they walked up the red carpet, smiling widely for the cameras. He managed to look doting as he stood back to allow the photographers to snap her dress. He kept his best knicker combusting smile on until they got inside, and away from the cameras.

"Wow, you are some actor," murmured Christina, impressed.

"You have no idea. Now, will you sit quietly and not bother me for the rest of the evening please. You need to stay next to me in case we are photographed, but if its all the same to you, I would rather not have to make small talk." He was matter of fact.

"Why are you being so mean? I didn't ask you to come with me. I was looking forward to an evening with Luke. It wouldn't hurt you to be nice. I was nice to you on James boat when you turned up with that old woman," she said, unaware of just how much of a nerve she was touching.

He didn't answer her. In truth he was white with fury and didn't trust himself to speak. He sat silently and blanked her all evening.

She sat and wondered what was up with him *probably gay'* she figured. "Ok gayboy, have it your way," was her parting shot as the limo dropped her home.

The following day, the gossip blogs were full of photos of the two of them. Dan explained the true situation to Lynne, and Harry yet again left a message on Dionne's phone.

CHAPTER 11

The Crystal Ball was quite a big deal. It was a fundraiser for several high profile homeless charities, and was held each year at the Royal Albert Hall. It was one of the rare events where the worlds of the city, celebrity, and academia came together to raise funds for those less fortunate. As such, it was a high profile event, attracting media from around the world to gawp at the great and good gathering for a party. Dionne had been a couple of times, but the publicity had been unwelcome. Now that she had dated a film star, she was more relaxed about appearing in the press, plus now that she wasn't trading, anonymity wasn't quite so necessary.

James picked her up in his limo, with a glass of Cristal waiting for her. They chatted easily, and swapped gossip during the journey to the venue. Dionne reflected on how relaxed she felt in James' company. He was urbane, funny, and wickedly intelligent. He also looked pretty damn good in his bespoke tux. She also reflected on how at ease he was with issues like her ever present security, as he lived a similar lifestyle to her.

They pulled up outside the Albert Hall, the waiting staff pulling open their doors. Dionne felt good in her Armani Prive dress and laboutins, although her dress felt a touch tight. She had teamed her outfit with a huge diamond lattice work necklace, and drop earrings. She knew James approved, he was a terrible show off, and would like a woman on his arm dripping in diamonds.

He placed his hand gently on the small of her back as they walked up the red carpet. Flashbulbs were going off all around them so fiercely she could barely see. Slightly disorientated, she looked up at James, he was gazing down at her, smiling. He grasped her waist a little tighter, and they walked into the venue.

He took two glasses of champagne from a passing waiter, and handed one to Dionne. Keeping his hand on the small of her back, they moved deeper into the Great Hall towards a group of hedge fund managers that James knew. Dionne stood at his side while they all chatted, listening to how boastful the men were about their piddly little funds.

'If only these little small dicked idiots knew who I am' she thought, smiling sweetly.

She was intrigued as to why James hadn't really introduced her properly, but was treating her a bit like he would a starlet or model.

She pushed the thought aside, and concentrated on listening properly to the fund manager's gossip, finding out that James had a large stake in the Jupiter one, she listened to the patter he was given regarding some share purchases made by the fund, wondering if she should mention that the companies P&L was pointing to the shares being overvalued, but decided to keep her mouth shut.

They were interrupted by Darren Karrett, "Dionne, hello, you're looking lovely this evening, noticed you're staying out of junk bonds, want to share the reason why?"

The rest of the men went quiet as they listened to this exchange.

"No big reason Darren, although I'm a bit concerned at the derivatives being traded on them. If that blows up when you're holding those bonds, then it's a wipeout," she asserted, suddenly aware that all the men had stopped talking and started listening.

"Are you in finance too?" A rotund, slightly sweaty man, standing next to James, asked her.

"Yes, although I don't hedge, my fund buys for long term growth," admitted Dionne, becoming aware that James was shifting uncomfortably beside her.

Darren was looking puzzled as he looked at James and her, trying to work out why nobody in the group appeared to know who she was. He decided to let it go and call her tomorrow, figuring that James must have good reason for being coy about his date. He parted with an "I'll call you."

Taking her hand, James led her from group to group, introducing her by just her first name, never mentioning her career. He kept away from people that Dionne knew, avoiding the groups he thought she might be friendly with. Dionne found it curious, but kept quiet, joining in the small talk, and listening to the finance talk.

During dinner, James boasted about his company, it's holdings, and how he had outwitted a currency dealer to make a huge profit. Dionne asked few questions, preferring to listen, amusing herself by calculating his net worth in her head.

James didn't donate during the auction, so Dionne stayed quiet, much to Darren's surprise. He watched the two of them closely, but seeing that Dionne looked relaxed, he turned his attention to the model who was his date that evening.

After dinner, James led Dionne onto the dance floor. He was a good dancer, albeit one with a slightly aggressive style. Being that close allowed Dionne to breathe his cologne. He smelt of Chanel and raw masculinity, a heady combination which made Dionne aware of his body moving against her. He felt strong and firm, his hand in hers felt soft and warm. She began to wonder what he'd be like in bed.

"Did I tell you how beautiful you look tonight?" Murmured James, gazing down at her with soft brown eyes. Dionne beamed up at him, delighted at the compliment.

"Thank you, and you look extremely handsome too," she breathed.

"Come home with me tonight?" He asked. She immediately thought of Harry.

' Well he played away, don't let him stop you Di, James is sex on legs, and it would serve Harry right'

She paused, "ok."

When the song finished, James grasped her hand and led her off the dance floor. He signalled to their security that they were leaving. Craig handed Dionne her wrap as James whisked her out the door.

"My security can take it from here," he said to Craig, who looked expectantly at Dionne.

"Yes that's fine," she confirmed.

James lived in a trophy house in Mayfair. It was all dark wood, glass and marble, an expensive and masculine space. He flung his jacket over the back of a chair, and wandered over to the kitchen area.

"Drink?" He asked

"Please," she replied, feeling nervous. James opened a bottle of Krug, and pulled two glasses out of a cupboard while Dionne examined the art on the walls. She was too busy looking at a Freud to notice James adding a tiny drop of ketamine to her drink. He handed her the glass while she examined a Hockney. He talked her through his art collection, explaining the artists and stories behind the pieces. She began to feel a touch tipsy, his deep, melodic voice washing over her as she stood. She felt the need to sit down. She placed her glass on the coffee table before slumping onto his sofa, feeling horribly out of control.

"Please get me home," she begged before passing out.

James carried her to a bedroom, and gently laid her down on a large iron framed four poster bed. He gently stripped her, folding her dress on the back of a chair carefully. Once she was naked, he took off her jewellery, and put it on a dressing table, next to her clutch bag. He raised her hands, and handcuffed her to the bedstead. He then covered her with the duvet, tucking her in, and left her to sleep it off.

James sat in his drawing room, his anticipation building. His big fantasy was kidnapping and torturing women. As most women threw themselves at him, and begged him not to leave them, it was a fantasy he didn't get to play out very often. Although he knew Dionne had agreed to come back with him, and clearly wanted him, the frisson of danger he felt at having her bound and helpless drove him almost mad with desire.

When she came to, she was naked in a large bed, her hands cuffed to the bedstead, and James was nowhere to be seen. She called out in a panic. James strode in,

"Calm down Di, your safe, I'm here," he said.

"Safe? I'm naked and handcuffed. Let me go this minute," she shouted, sending a shiver of excitement down his spine.

"We haven't had our fun yet, and I know you want me, I most certainly want you, I just have particular tastes," he crooned, "this is how I want to make love, I want you bound up, helpless and needing me. If you're a good lover, I'll let you fuck me again afterwards with your hands untied."

James ran his hands down her naked body, touching her almost reverently, never taking his eyes off her. She watched as he stripped off his clothes quickly, revealing a smaller than expected penis. Cupping both breasts, he kissed her face chastely, before stroking her hair. Suddenly he gripped a handful of hair and tugged it hard, causing her to cry out in pain and fear.

"I think you like a bit of pain," he whispered, "I bet it turns you on."

"No," she whimpered, "I don't like pain. It doesn't do it for me."

He laughed. "Well I do, and right now I have the advantage. I know you want me to fuck you, you flirted all night, playing the dirty girl. So the deal is that you do this for me, and I'll fuck you till you come."

'Oh great, a pervert, ok play along and get out alive' she thought.

"What do you want me to do?" She asked.

"Turn over," he ordered, before flipping her onto her front, and tying a gag round her mouth. He pulled her hips up roughly and slowly fondled her buttocks. She cringed.

Whack! He brought a crop down on her bare buttock. She jumped from the noise and the shock of the pain. He brought it down again and again, watching her squirming on the bed, fear and shock on her face. After several minutes he dropped the crop, and caressed her sore arse, running his hands over the red welts.

"Oh baby, you did so well," he said softly, giving Dionne a glimmer of hope her ordeal was over.

"Just a bit more, it turns me on so much," he said ominously, reaching under the bed for a flogger. Dionne screwed her eyes shut, and braced herself for the onslaught. When it came, it took her breath away. Blows rained down across her back, biting and searing her soft skin. She tried to cry out, but the gag silenced her. She lost track of how long he hit her for, unsure if she passed out again from the ketamine, or just blocked out the pain he was inflicting on her.

He stopped, dropping the flogger on the floor. "Such a good girl, I'm gonna give you what you want now," he murmured, sliding on a condom. He pulled her hips back up, and crammed his cock into her anus. Her eyes pinged open, pain, fear and shock on her face as he humped her. He reached round and roughly rubbed her dry clitoris causing her to try and cry out again in more pain.

Thankfully he came quickly, shuddering as his orgasm tore through him. He collapsed on her welt ridden back, pressing her into the bed.

Abruptly, he withdrew, pulling the condom off his short penis, and dropping it on the floor. He untied her gag, and unlocked the handcuffs. He tried to rub her shoulder, but stopped when she flinched. When she sat up, he stared at her uncertainly.

"That was amazing Di, you are so sexy," he said softly.

"Covered in welts, snot coming out my nose and blood from my arse, yeah right. Get me a taxi and my dress you bastard."

He looked perplexed. "Didn't you enjoy it?" He asked, seemingly confused.

"Are you mad? No I fucking didn't." She spotted her dress across the room and ran over to grab it and pull it on. He watched wide eyed as she stuffed her jewellery in her handbag, grabbed her shoes, and ran for it.

"Dionne, wait," she heard him call behind her, panic evident in his voice. She ran full pelt down the stairs, and out the front door.

James was sitting on his bed, unable to run after her due to his nakedness. He had been so sure she would love the whole dominance scenario, most of the women he bedded had said they loved it.

'Christina had practically begged for more, so why had this one run off in a huff?' He thought, unable to fathom what had gone wrong. He debated calling her, but figured it best to write her off as incompatible.

Dionne had flagged down a taxi outside, and was on her way home. The taxi driver had asked her if she was ok, mainly because she was sobbing, snotty, and had smeared makeup all over her face. Mercifully, the ride home was short, and she had called ahead to ensure the gates were opened.

Once home, she ran past Connor and went straight to her bedroom. She crawled into her bed and sobbed. Every part of her hurt. She felt sick, she ached, and she felt humiliated. She just about made it to the bathroom before throwing up.

'The bastard must have drugged me'

She called Lynne, but all she could manage between sobs was "help."

She tried to shower, but the water felt like hot needles. Her back was a mass of red, swollen welts. She discovered a cool bath soothed and calmed the pain, but nothing could wash away the humiliation she felt.

Lynne made it back in sixteen hours of Dionne's call, taking a private jet back to London. She listened wide eyed to the story, and whistled through her teeth at the injuries.

"I don't know what to say Di, I would never have expected that of James either. I'm so sorry this happened. Are you gonna report him?"

"No point, I was there voluntarily, he will just claim it was consensual."

In the days that followed, Lynne applied calamine lotion to the welts, listened as Dionne ranted and cried, and held her hair back as she threw up.

After three days, the welts had faded, the throwing up hadn't.

"Made you an appointment with Dr Radley this afternoon," announced Lynne.

"Ok," muttered Dionne, feeling ropey.

"Do you want me to call Harry?" asked Lynne.

'Yes, oh yes please, I need him' she thought.

"No I'll be fine," she said.

Meanwhile in LA, Harry was staring at his laptop in a sick, jealous fury. He was looking at pictures of Dionne and James arriving at the crystal ball, captioned with 'Is this the new power couple?' The tears ran unchecked down his cheeks as he finally gave in to his grief.

Harry had never loved a woman before, let alone loved and lost. He was barely functioning, struggling with his lines, looking so rough that the makeup artists were having to practically airbrush him, and generally being depressed. His distress was compounded when he found out that Lynne had been pulled back to London by a strange, panicked phone call from Dionne.

'What the hell is going on there? Is she ok? Is something wrong?'

He wondered.

He racked his brains trying to think of a scenario that Dionne couldn't cope with alone, and drew a blank. He called Dan to see if he had any news.

"All Lynne's told me is that there was an incident involving Dionne. No details. Have you tried to call?"

"Not in the last couple of days. I will try again though. Let me know if you find out anything yeah?"

"Will do, and Harry? Tell her about the club."

"Speak to you soon, bye." Harry cut the call. Taking a deep breath, he dialled Dionne's number.

"Hi Harry," a small voice answered, taking him by surprise.

"Dionne, oh thank god you answered, are you ok?"

"No, I got attacked, I'm ok though, nothing life threatening, I'm just shaken up."

"Where were your security?" Harry asked, perplexed.

"It's a long story, not one for a phone call."

Harry considered his options. It would cause a massive problem for him to drop everything and go to London. "Do you want me to come to London?" He heard a snuffle.

"You would still do that for me?" She said in a small voice.

"Of course I would. Just say the word and I'll get there. Baby I miss you so much, and I'd do anything for you, you know that." The little crack in his voice betrayed his emotion.

"Will you tell me the truth about that club?"

Harry sucked in a deep breath. "Yes, I will, but not on the phone."

"I'll be over in about sixteen hours. I make that seven o clock LA time. Meet me at the house? I need your arms around me." Dionne snuffled some more, which made his heart break.

"Oh baby I can't wait to see you, and I'll hold you as tight as you want," said Harry, relief flooding through him.

"I'll make arrangements and get on a plane. If I can be any quicker, I will."

"Ok baby, I love you."

"Love you too," said Dionne without hesitation.

"Lynne, cancel the doctor, we're off to LA," hollered Dionne. Lynne popped her head round the door.

"Well you sound perkier. Spoken to Harry I presume?" Lynne smirked knowingly.

"Yes. I just booked a flight. You have precisely ten minutes to get your shoes on and grab your handbag and passport." Dionne replied, having perked up considerably. Within ten minutes they were out the door and on their way.

As Dionne got out of the car outside her LA house, Harry came out of the front door. She threw herself into his arms, and breathed in his wonderful scent. Finally feeling safe again, she began to cry. Harry held her tight, letting her cry into his chest. When her sobbing subsided, he picked her up and carried her inside, taking her straight up to her bedroom. He fetched some tissues from the bathroom so he could dry her tears, and wipe her nose. The sight of her gentle, caring man, calmly looking after her, made her cry again. He held her tight in his muscular, strong arms, ignoring the wet, slightly snotty patch forming on his t shirt.

Eventually she stopped crying. He went down to the kitchen and brought them each back a cup of coffee, which they sat silently drinking. When she had composed herself, she told him what had happened. His face turned ashen.

"I want to kill him," said Harry when she had finished.

"I want to do more than that," she replied. "I want to bankrupt him, and I will. I warn you now Harry, this is going to be a side of me that I hoped you would never see. By the time I'm finished with him, he'll be in a council flat on benefits. That would hurt him far more than a quick death."

Harry looked deep into her eyes. "Do your worst," he said.

"Now it's your turn to do some explaining," said Dionne. Harry lay down on the bed, and stared at the pillow, not wanting to look at her. He began.

"I think I got stuck emotionally at age six, when Mum died. When things got difficult or stressful I used to go back to age 5 in my head. I used to do things that reminded me of a time when I felt loved and happy. When I discovered that I had sexual problems with women, I began to look around for alternatives. You may have heard of the term 'adult baby', I'm not one of those, don't panic," he said hastily. "There is a genre of that called 'kidults' though, which is people who like to retreat into their childhood selves. I found out about The Chamber through an online forum. They have rooms that cater for people like me. I dress like a five year old, play, watch cartoons, and become five years old again. I don't wear a nappy or anything gross like that though," he added.

"So why the shame and secrecy?" Probed Dionne.

"Because I masturbate there. The Mama who looks after the nursery doesn't touch me, I do it myself. It's a bit of a sick thing to have to admit to," he confessed.

"So let me get this straight, you dress up, play with toys, and have a wank?" She asked in a calm voice.

Harry nodded. "That's the sum of it. I'm sorry Di, I know it's bad, and I'm sure you didn't expect that." He couldn't meet her eyes. She sat silently, trying to take it all in. He willed her to say something.

Dionne took a deep breath. "Why the masturbation?" ·

"I don't know. I think I just felt a bit stupid going to a sex club and not doing anything but play. The Mama just strokes my head, nothing else."

"Has she ever done more for you?"

"No, I don't actually go there for sex, it just fulfils some sort of need in me. It's hard to put into words," he paused, "are you totally disgusted with me?"

She gazed at his beautiful, anxious face and pulled him into her arms, holding him tight.

"Baby it's okay. I was worried you were whipping people there. I'm not shocked or disgusted, I'm just relieved that's all you're doing. I just don't know why you couldn't have told me before."

"I felt ashamed of needing it, and pretty stupid to be honest. I must look quite daft in my kid stuff, all six foot one of me. I worried you would think I was a weirdo, or I had a mother complex."

Dionne stared into his expressive eyes, not quite able to believe that this intensely masculine man was really a scared, lost little boy who had to return to five years old every now and again to be able to live his life. Aware of how much he had bared, her heart broke for him.

He broke her reverie. "Can I see what that bastard did to your back?"

She pulled off her shirt and showed him her back. It had calmed down significantly, only the red marks remaining.

"The swelling's gone down now. Lynne has been dousing me with calamine lotion twice a day since she got back. It was pretty horrific four days ago," she explained.

Harry closed his eyes in fury, trying not to allow Dionne see his anger. He couldn't allow himself to picture her beautiful body being defiled in that way.

Opening his eyes, he gently touched her back. "Does it still hurt?"

"It's still tender, but the burning has gone. It just feels bruised now. It feels better now you're stroking it," she admitted, seeing the anger and disgust written all over his lovely face.

"I will always be gentle with you, I can promise you that," he said, repeating what he had said on their first date.

"And I will always be gentle with you too, especially with your heart," she replied, kissing the tip of his nose.

"And my dick I hope," laughed Harry.

With the telling of secrets out of the way, they headed downstairs to find Lynne and Dan. They didn't discuss Dionne's ordeal, or Harry's secret, preferring to keep the mood lighter. They laughed at Dan's description of his horrible costume, and Harry's drug addled leading lady. Harry told them all about his evening escorting Christina, and her less than complimentary parting words, which made Dionne giggle.

After a great meal, and a couple of bottles of good wine, they all turned in for the night. Dionne led Harry to their room, clasping his hand firmly, aware that he wouldn't see sleeping together as a foregone conclusion.

He got into bed first, and held his arms open for her. She slid straight into them, and rested her head on his chest, listening to his heartbeat.

"I'm sorry," she said.

"What for?" He asked, puzzled.

"For thinking he would be able to replace you," she sighed.

"Well I'm sorry too."

"For?"

"Thinking that being without you would be easier than telling you the truth," he said quietly.

"Was it?"

"No, being without you nearly broke me. I don't think I've ever been in so much pain," he admitted, sadness evident in his voice.

She lifted her head, and kissed him softly. He deepened the kiss, tugging her to lay completely flush against him. He fisted his hands in her hair, wanting to avoid her tender back, but needing to touch her. She ran her hands over his shoulders, sliding over his muscular chest, basking in his warmth. She lowered her hands to stroke his erection with the softest, most featherlight touch.

Their lovemaking was slow and gentle that night, reflecting their need to make amends, and demonstrate their affection, neither one wanting to speed or lose control.

Harry watched her as she climaxed, straddling him, gazing at her with pure adoration on his face. Afterwards, he wrapped himself around her, holding her until they both fell asleep.

The two men went to work the next day, leaving Dionne and Lynne sitting by the pool.

"So what was Harry's big secret?" Lynne asked, sipping her latte. Dionne hadn't discussed with Harry what to tell Lynne. She decided to be honest.

"He dressed as a child, played with toys and wanked himself off there," she blurted out, cringing slightly, expecting Lynne to laugh.

"That all? I was expecting much worse," said Lynne dismissively.

"Me too. No idea why he didn't just come clean."

Lynne snorted at the double entendre, then coughed as her coffee went down the wrong pipe. They both giggled.

"Does this mean we are both here for the foreseeable? Only I will need to get us both more clothes. I've only got a few outfits here, and you're not much better off." Lynne pointed out.

"Oh, yeah, would you mind?" Said Dionne, knowing full well her friend would be delighted. "I think I put on a bit of weight though, some of my clothes are feeling a bit tight, I need to cut down for a week or so."

"Hmm, we should change to skinny lattes, can't have you getting fat," agreed Lynne. She went on, "any thoughts on teaching James a lesson, or are you gonna let it go?"

"Forming plans. I'm going to be working out here, aiming to teach him a lesson he won't forget. Actually I'm gonna break his balls. I'm gonna be pretty busy for a while playing financial chess, so can you look after everything else for me?"

"Of course. Does Harry know the evil master of the universe is gonna rear her ugly head, and he'll have a ringside seat? You need to warn him. I've seen you like it, and it ain't pretty, in fact you're rather terrifying when you're full on." Said Lynne fondly.

CHAPTER 12

Ensconced in her office, Dionne called Darren. "Hi Darren, how are you? Sorry didn't get to chat to you at the ball."

"Hello Dionne, yes that was rather a strange evening. Don't think James quite liked you being the senior partner. Those hedge funders seemed surprised that you were in the business too. Would at least have expected him to introduce you properly," replied Darren, pleased to be given the chance to stick the boot in. He had never like James Rankin, and the fact that he had pulled Dionne had pissed him off.

"That's why I'm calling you. James beat seven bells out of me that night. I need your help."

"What physically? He hit you? Please tell me that's not what you mean," whispered Darren, appalled.

"Yep, drugged me, beat me and raped me. I'm in LA at the moment. I had to get away from London."

Darren whistled through his teeth. "I've heard rumours about him over the years, but wouldn't have expected him to pull shit like that with someone like you. Di, I'm so sorry to hear this. Now what do you need me to do?" Dionne outlined her plans, arranging to fly Darren over to LA two days later. He was in.

She spent the rest of the day talking to fellow financiers. People who John and her had known and dealt with over the years, and who could be trusted. She sat back and reflected on the legacy John had left her. Good friends who wanted to help her, who trusted her business acumen, who would all fly out to LA at the drop of a hat, just as she would for them. She would break James Rankin if it was the last thing she did.

She called Adam Fairchild and asked him for everything he could dig up on James, his business dealings and his personal life. Finally she sat and listed out all his investments that he had boasted about that terrible evening, and formed plans to ruin him.

Harry arrived home from the studio at six, delighted to be spending the evening with Dionne, and the luxurious surroundings of Bel Air. Her staff had organised the move out of his third world apartment, and into the lush oasis that she called home.

He grabbed a beer from the kitchen before hunting her down. He found her in her office, typing furiously while watching a monitor that appeared to show data from the New York stock exchange.

"Hey baby, how was your day?" He asked as he bent down to kiss her.

"Productive," she replied absentmindedly, pressing 'send' on her keyboard. "Sorry darling, how was yours?" She asked, remembering her manners.

"Best day for ages. Lots of one take scenes today. I seem to be back in the zone," he beamed.

"Good, listen, we have some visitors coming this week, five of them. We will be holding a meeting here. It's completely secret, nothing must get out. You ok with that?"

"Sure, who's coming?" He asked, intrigued.

"Five masters of the universe. Seriously, five other financiers. They are all going to be assisting me in the downfall of James Rankin," she explained.

"Why would they do that?"

"I've helped them with similar issues in the past. Remember Lehmans? We did that. The CEO shafted George Boros in a securitised debt deal, so we got together and bankrupted them." She shrugged.

"So you will all get together and bankrupt the bastard? How will you do it?" Asked Harry, his eyes widening.

"We all have an area of expertise. Between the six of us, we pretty much cover all angles of finance, for instance, Darren covers shares and hedge funds, George deals currency, Alex derivatives, etc. We each work on our own areas to bring about the result we want."

"So what's your area of expertise Di?"

"I'm the chess player, it's my job to be three steps ahead of everyone else."

'Jesus, she's scary when she's angry' he thought, glad he wasn't on the receiving end this time.

Dionne worked through the evening, pausing only to quickly eat. Harry played tennis with Lynne, and then sat in his pants watching telly, quite happy. Before he headed up to bed, he called into the office to tell Dionne it was eleven o'clock, and he was gonna shower and turn in.

"Oh darling, I'm sorry, I didn't mean to ignore you. Let me switch off and I'll join you," she said, aware that she needed to give him some attention too.

"Not a problem baby, I can see you're busy. Would you prefer me to run you a bath?"

"A shower sounds good. I'll be there in two minutes." She switched off her screens, and followed Harry upstairs.

Harry soaped her all over, which, after a day spent staring at screens, was just what she needed. She let out a large sigh. Seeing her body relax, he began to shampoo her hair, his firm fingers almost sending her into a coma. After he combed conditioner through, she returned the favour, massaging his shoulders as she lathered up his body wash. His body felt hard and strong underneath her hands, not betraying the soft, vulnerable man below.

"Harry."

"Hmm?"

"Make me scream tonight?" He opened his eyes to see her hopeful face smiling at him.

"Your wish is my command, what's brought this on? I thought you were tired."

"I'm a bit amped up, I need to release some tension," she admitted.

He flicked off the shower, and grabbed a towel, which he wrapped round his hips. He took another, and began to dry her, paying particular attention to the area between her legs. After a few minutes he dropped all pretence of drying her off, and just ran his fingers rhythmically over her clit, feeling her arousal.

He carried her to the bed, sitting her on the edge. He laid her back and slammed into her, pulling her feet up to his shoulders. He pumped into her, changing angles to rub his wide cock over her g spot. Grabbing her vibrator, he pressed it onto her clitoris, her garbled shouts confirming he was getting it right.

"Harder, please harder," she cried, spurring him on. He grasped her hips to increase his thrusts, feeling her wetness on him as he pushed her towards her climax. She came with a loud scream, rippling around him, causing him to spurt hotly inside her.

He flopped down onto the bed beside her, both of them slicked in sweat and breathing heavily.

"Not too rough for you?" He asked, not looking at her.

"Oh god no, it was delicious." She smiled. "Certainly took care of that tension."

"Why is it that whenever we make love, it makes me more horny?" He mused before pouncing on her and running his tongue over her nipple.

"Another hard fuck? I am such a lucky girl," she giggled, grabbing his cock ring and anal vibrator out of the drawer. Harry's eyes glittered at the sight of them.

"You want a hard fuck? Shall I pound you on your back? Or doggy style," he asked, cocking his head to one side.

"Oh on my back, I want to see your face when you come," she purred, as she gently inserted his vibrator.

(They had discovered that as soon as it was switched on, Harry's cock would get stone hard, and leak Pre-cum)

He positioned himself on top of her, and enthusiastically fucked her hard until they both shouted their release.

With all her tension taken care of, Dionne rolled onto her side, and promptly fell asleep.

The next day, Harry arrived home from work to find her working in her office, surrounded by spreadsheets and papers.

"Hi darling, good day?" Dionne asked absentmindedly.

"Fine thanks, did another fight scene today, the extras....." Harry droned on for ten minutes before he realised she wasn't listening. "You're not listening to a word of this are you?"

"Eh? Oh sorry darling, I'm trying to analyse all this before the others get here. I need to have the analysis and strategy ready for them. Can you look after yourself this evening? I think Lynne and Dan are around somewhere." She smiled up at his disgruntled face.

"Ok, I'll leave you to it. Anything you want?"

"Coffee please."

Harry wandered out of her study, wondering what to do for the evening. He ordered her coffee, and went up to his dressing room to get changed into a pair of shorts. After doing several lengths of the pool, he dried off, and wandered into the games room.

'How did I ever think call of duty was exciting? He mused, missing her company as he tried to get into the game. He abandoned it after half an hour, preferring to wander around the grounds thinking.

'I wonder if this is it, if she's the love of my life. Does she feel as much for me as I feel for her? Can I fit into her world? Would she make me give up my career? I would for her. Does she just want me for sex? She says she loves me, so I don't think it is just the sex. Can we really make this last forever, I don't want to go back to life alone now.'

Harry's musings raised more questions than they answered. He resolved to talk to Dionne once her guests had gone.

The next day, their guests arrived, each flying in by private jet. They were met by limousines with tinted windows, and whisked quickly to Dionne's mansion. Dionne greeted each man with a handshake and a kiss as they arrived, before the staff showed each man to a suite to freshen up ready for their meeting.

At three o'clock, they all met in the dining room, greeting each other as old friends. Once drinks were served, they settled down to business. Dionne stood to address the room.

"Gentlemen, thank you all for coming today. I have explained the nature of the situation to each of you prior to your arrival, so I suggest we can skip running through it again. My security expert has been digging out details on Mr Rankin, and his investments." Dionne passed a small file to each of the five men. "As you can see, his holdings are quite diversified, but I've identified a number of Achilles heels in his investment strategies, primarily his use of hedge funds, and spread bets." She passed round another sheet of paper.

The men all sat and read the file and the sheet. Darren spoke first. "The Jupiter fund has a weakness in their shareholding of tech stocks.

They bought at the top, if I crash that market, especially if I can catch them on the wrong side of a hedge, I can break that fund fairly easily."

"Great, so George, what can you do with his currency holdings?" She said, looking at Mr Boros expectantly.

He smiled. "I can feel a run on the yen coming. Although if he has any sense he will pull out before he's lost the lot."

"Agreed, but where will he put it?" Prompted Dionne, looking at Alexander Renoux.

"Into a spread bet to gain from the movements of course, which is where we all join together. How much is the war chest, because we will have to swing the market incredibly quickly," pointed out Alexander.

"I have 48 billion in cash. Although I'd rather not use it all up," said Dionne, noticing blinks of astonishment around the table. The men each pledged amounts running into billions for the project's war chest.

"I will be on hand to assist James in liquidating assets to pay for his misadventures in spread betting," asserted Sheik Diwarni. "Anyone want his yacht? At cost of course."

The men all chuckled.

"I wouldn't mind it," piped up Darren, to much laughter.

"His art collection isn't bad. I'll have that off you," smirked Dionne.

The fifth and final man at the table spoke. "If you pull this off Di, you will end up making the six of us a few billion each. I think you will get the art as a prize. Now before we commence, how far do we go? Leave him a few million or totally bust?"

Dionne looked at the sultan with amusement. "Totally, utterly broke."

They spent another couple of hours discussing the minutiae of the strategy, the older, wise, financiers adding suggestions to Dionne to speed, or foolproof her strategy further.

Harry arrived home at half six to find Dionne and five men leaving the dining room. She introduced him proudly to everyone, and herded them all out to the terrace for drinks before dinner.

Much to Harry's surprise, they were good company, chatting happily about their wives and families. Darren asked Harry for a game of tennis, which everyone watched until dinner was announced.

They all ate informally on the terrace. George telling funny stories about Dionne as a 'youngster', making them all laugh. Harry was struck by how much genuine affection there was for Dionne from the group, and how powerful the gathering was. All the men present were moguls, people who shaped the financial world, and his girlfriend was at the centre of it.

The sheik leaned over to Harry, and spoke quietly, "Were you aware that Dionne was a part of this?" He indicated around the table.

"Not really," admitted Harry, "I knew she was a financier, and obviously she's very wealthy, but no idea she was up there with all of you."

The sheik chuckled, "In cash terms, she is the wealthiest of all of us. Dionne is the arch strategist, we all admire her. I'm glad she has a caring man to look after her though Harry. Even a mistress of the universe needs a mortal to love, and especially after this disaster with the unpleasant Mr Rankin."

"I want to rip that bastard limb from limb," muttered Harry, clenching his fists.

"I wouldn't worry about that, when we have done with him, he will be, how do I say it?, Neutered," laughed The Sheik.

The remainder of the evening was awash with fine wine, good food, and great conversation with fascinating people. Seeing Dionne in her element, surrounded by intelligent people, enchanted Harry. He clapped, along with the others, when old George Boras made Dionne do her party trick of 'beat the calculator', prompting a little blush from her.

The following day, they all returned home, with the plan scheduled to begin the following day. Once Dionne had prepared everything ready for the start, she decided to take the rest of the afternoon off.

Lynne had laid low while the financiers were around. Sheik Diwarni had a bit of a crush on her, and he tended to get a bit maudlin after a drink, so she had stayed out of sight.

The two women met in the pool that afternoon, enjoying a leisurely swim before having some G&T's, and a gossip.

Lynne and Dan's relationship was going from strength to strength, so much so, that she confided to Dionne that she had come off the pill, and was convinced he was going to propose fairly soon.

"How do you feel about me getting married and having babies Di?"

"Delighted, you deserve to be happy, and Dan makes you happy. It would be quite nice to have some little ones around. They won't be coming from me, so you better get a move on and pop a few out," said Dionne, teasing.

"Do you think Harry will propose?"

"Doubt it, he's a bit sensitive about the whole gold digger label," said Dionne, a sad tinge to her voice. "Does Dan know about your money?" Dionne had lodged fifty million in Lynne's account a few years previously to make her feel more secure about not pursuing a career.

"Yes, he's not exactly poor himself, so it's been a non issue."

"Good, I'll keep my fingers crossed for you."

"How did Harry get along with the moguls?" enquired Lynne.

"Surprisingly well," said Dionne, "he seemed to enjoy their company, and he didn't seem fazed at all."

"Maybe you don't give him enough credit sometimes. He's not just a pretty face," chided Lynne, gently.

Dan and Harry were in Van Cleef looking at rings, having both left work early. Dan had made the decision to propose to Lynne soon, and wanted Harry to help him choose a great engagement ring. The sales assistant was a kindly looking middle aged man, who ushered them both through to a private room, and arranged for an assortment of rings to be brought through to show them.

"Sir, this tray has a selection of white diamonds, in various cuts. Do you have an idea of what you are looking for? Or is there anything the lady has indicated that she likes?" The jeweller asked.

Dan perused the tray, picking up a princess cut diamond ring.

"She doesn't wear any rings, so I don't really know what her taste is. I think she wears platinum rather than gold though."

The jeweller took the tray, and replaced it with a selection of platinum set rings. "A diamond should speak to you sir, rest assured that all these diamonds are white flawless, top quality, and among the best in the world, so concentrate on finding the one that communicates how you feel about her," he advised.

"Anything larger?" Dan asked. The jeweller took the tray and disappeared for a few minutes. He returned with another tray, flanked by a security guard.

"These are the largest stones we have that are already set. If you want anything larger, it would have to be sourced, cut and set to order." He stepped back to allow the two men to examine the contents of the tray. Dan immediately picked up an emerald cut diamond ring, with smaller diamonds set around the outside. He stared hard at it, slipping it on the end of his pinky.

"This is the one," he said decisively.

"A good choice sir." The jeweller said.

Harry sat looking at the rings. "Do you think I should choose one for Di while we're here?"

"You planning on proposing too then?" Dan looked shocked.

"Maybe. Might be an idea to have one ready, just in case," hedged Harry, blushing slightly. He picked up a simple oval diamond ring. The stone was large, and set simply on a plain platinum band.

"This is the one. How much is it?" He asked the jeweller.

"Four million dollars sir."

"I'll take it." Harry gulped slightly.

They paid for the rings and headed back to the house, both slightly dazed at spending so much in one afternoon. Harry stuffed the small box into his sock drawer, hiding it at the back, hoping it wouldn't be there for long.

Harry pretended to arrive home from the studio exhausted. They had been filming a complicated action scene that morning, which the extras had kept screwing up. He said he was tired, pissed off and a bit beaten up. He found Dionne sitting by the pool with Lynne, laughing over something.

Flopping down on a sun lounger, he moaned about his day, how demanding the director was, and how tiring it had all been. Dionne listened politely.

"...and it was so hot, waiting around for the choreographer to go over the fight scene YET again, well I sweated through three lots of makeup. Had to practically chisel it off myself. Oh, where are the moguls?"

"Gone. We start tonight due to time zones. I'm gonna be round the clock for the next week or so, you'll just have to bear with me a bit." Warned Dionne.

"Sure, no problem, just tell me when you need me to leave you alone," said Harry, sincerely.

Lynne snorted."Think you'll spot it Harry, she turns into a monster. When she's peaking, you will be way too scared to go within ten feet of that study. Don't forget, I've seen it when they do this stuff, and it ain't pretty."

Harry stared at his dainty little blonde lover, completely unable to imagine her being a monster. A bit blunt maybe, and he'd seen her angry, but nothing horrific.

"Hmm, I'll believe it when I see it."

That night, Harry slept alone. Dionne was positioning investments on the sly, and due to the time difference, it meant she had to work overnight. He assumed she would get some sleep during the day while he was at work.

By the third night, he was hearing yelling coming from her office. He padded down to investigate, and found her punching the air and yelling at the screens.

"YES! Darren managed to crash the footsie, and eight hedge funds have gone bust including Jupiter as a result. Alex has picked up the baton now. George is currently wiping out the yen, followed by the euro. He won't fucking know what's hit him. I'm giving him nowhere to turn." She shouted, her eyes sparkling.

Harry stood open mouthed. Despite knowing little about stocks and shares, he didn't think crashing markets could be a good thing, and he had been reading the headlines about the terrible financial crisis sweeping the world.

"What about the effects of this on everyone else?" He asked, appalled at her aggression.

She looked at Harry as if he had grown two heads. "Just a bit of collateral damage. It's fine, we'll put things back as soon as we're done. I'll even donate some to charity if you want," she muttered.

Harry kissed her briefly, and padded back to bed, noticing it was three in the morning. He lay awake, contemplating how his dainty, ladylike girlfriend had morphed into a nocturnal monster, who was currently stamping on the world financial systems.

The following night, Dionne got a call from the Sheik, "I just bought his yacht for twenty million, his house for five million, and his art collection for thirty million. He is clearly desperate for cash."

She grinned, knowing full well he would risk it as a last throw of the dice. "Does he have any idea this is linked to me?" She asked.

"Yes. He asked if I'd seen you, of course I said not, but he is not a stupid man, and he has seen the market move against him on every investment he had."

She sat back and contemplated James next move. "My guess is that if he's figured this out, he will hide his last bit of money behind me. He knows I have a majority share in Universal, so will try and protect his money that way. Can I suggest you all get out of Universal before I fuck it over."

'Harry will not be pleased if I have to do that'

"I will communicate that to the others, oh and Di, you're doing great," he said before he cut the call.

Meanwhile in London, James was ranting at Darren in The Wolsley. Darren had invited James to lunch on the pretence of discussing a new fund. James was delighted, the past few days had been hellish.

"Are you in contact with the Devere bitch? I swear to god she's behind these market swings," he almost shouted.

Darren regarded James closely, he looked like shit, which was very unlike James, and was clearly under pressure. "I don't think 'the Devere bitch' as you so eloquently put it, is even in London, let alone trading. Last time I heard from her was last year on a junk bond deal. I might add that she fucked me over on that deal somewhat. I thought you had designs on her, escorting her to the ball, what happened? Did she say no?" Darren said, sneering slightly, to keep up pretence.

"She was begging me for it, I said no actually, too old for me."

Darren inwardly rolled his eyes, but wanted to keep James talking. He had spotted James' tell. The little sign he was lying. James had rubbed his chin.

"So you didn't move fast enough with these mad markets?" Probed Darren.

Rub rub, "Oh yes, I made a packet out of it all. I want to streamline some of my holdings though, so I'm looking for a safe place for thirty mill right now," rub rub, "and I'm thinking of moving, somewhere warmer than this shithole, so I need an investment that will pay a dividend for some income." rub rub.

Darren tried not to laugh. He knew full well that James had sold everything to the sheik at a knockdown price to cover losses on a spread bet. He would call Dionne with the news that James was down to thirty mill, if that, and that he thought she was behind it all.

"You could try a spread bet to recoup some money, the euro is gonna continue falling. I saw the preliminary company reports for some of the biggest firms in the zone, and it ain't pretty" tipped Darren, tapping the side of his nose, and apparently giving out insider information.

"Thanks mate, may just do that. All or nothing right?" sighed James.

"Right," agreed Darren, changing the subject to the new investment fund he was allegedly considering. He listened to James' ideas during lunch, politely paying the bill before he left.

Back in his office, Darren communicated the encounter to Dionne. She immediately checked out the list of universal shareholders. Straight away she spotted J Rankin listed as buying just over twenty three million shares that day. She checked the share price, *'so he spent fifteen million'* she thought. *'Bingo, he split the investment. He bet on the euro too.'*

The communication went out to the group of six to move the euro price upwards fast. They all piled in, making the currency shoot up, their combined fire power totally overwhelming the central bank's ability to control things.

James sat in his hotel room, staring at his laptop in disbelief. He watched as his remaining money had disappeared in a flash, followed by heavy losses at being on the wrong side of the bet without a stop. Within the space of a week, he was broke.

He sold the shares he stashed in universal to pay part of his debt, but by that time he was facing losses of a further eight million pounds. With no assets left apart from his clothes and laptop, he couldn't even pay his hotel bill.

'May as well enjoy my last day of luxury' he thought, as he ordered a Kobe beef steak, and a bottle of Chateaux Margaux from room service.

He ate his meal in a daze, wallowing in self pity at having both made, and lost a fortune. He contemplated having to find somewhere to stay, having sold his house, and his yacht, and realised he had no actual friends he could call upon. He also knew it was only a matter of time until The Sheik discovered his secrets.

Unable to face the shame of bankruptcy, poverty, and exposure, he took a handgun out of his briefcase and calmly blew his brains out.

The news reached Dionne at midday LA time, causing her to jump for joy. After congratulatory phone calls from the group, she spent the afternoon righting the markets, and pulling her cash back out. They all agreed to meet up that weekend to share out the spoils and have a drink. The week had been intense for all of them, so they all needed to relax.

She was still hyper when Harry arrived home. She danced round happily as she gave him the news until she became aware he wasn't dancing along with her.

"Harry, what's up, you wanted to rip him apart if I recall," she reminded him.

"I know, it's just, I dunno, I can't believe you did it," he replied.

"I did tell you I would. Did you think I couldn't?"

"I didn't really think you could swing world markets, no, so forgive me for being a bit awed at my scary girlfriend," he smiled, "I truly had no idea you held so much....power," he said, scrabbling to find the right words.

"Speaking of power, I really need one of your hard fucks right now. Winning makes me as horny as hell," she demanded, dragging him towards the stairs. He picked her up and flung her over his shoulder, carrying her caveman style to the bedroom.

She practically ripped his clothes off, and seeing how turned on she was, he wasted no time slamming into her. She begged him to fuck her harder as he pounded into her, which spurred him on. Hearing her shout her release, he let go, collapsing onto her as he came.

"I needed that," purred Dionne. Harry lay on the bed trying to get his breath back. Dionne had been like a ravenous beast, which he had never seen before. He was used to her being dainty and loving, not demanding and dominant. It disquieted him. He buried the thought, hopeful that James' death had brought the episode to an end, and he would have his sweet, funny Dionne back.

They shared a shower, soaping each other and washing each other's hair. He could feel the tension leaving Dionne's shoulders as he massaged her. Dionne kissed Harry, desperate to reconnect with him. She reasoned that living with a nocturnal bitch who wreaked havoc on the world indices, couldn't have been much fun.

"Did it shock you that I was such a vengeful bitch?" Dionne asked, as she wanted to address the issue.

"Yes. I won't lie, I was surprised. I don't really see you that way. Just hope I'm never on the receiving end. Theres one thing that I haven't worked out though."

"What's that," she asked, curious.

"Why you did nothing to me when you left me over the nursery," he said, looking her straight in the eyes.

"Because I love you. James hurt me, physically and mentally. You broke my heart. There's a big difference."

"How is that different?"

"I had no feelings for James, apart from hatred after what he did. I still loved you, even after what you did, I just wanted you to love me back as much. I had no desire for retribution, even though I could have. You don't damage the things you love do you?"

He turned to gaze at her, unable to comprehend his good fortune in finding her. He knew she could have wrecked his career, yet she did nothing, despite her obvious pain in catching him coming out of The Chamber.

'She loves me' the realisation hit him.

'If I propose I'm a gold digger, if I don't, she may think I don't want her after she screwed James over. What to do?' He thought.

"Right now I'm just happy that you're back in my life. I need to become the man who deserves you Di," he said thoughtfully. "Dans told me he wants to propose to Lynne, do you think she'll say yes?" He asked.

"I think she'll bite his hand off," Dionne laughed. "She told me she's hoping he'll ask her. First time for everything I suppose, I just didn't think she'd ever find 'the one', so it's lovely to see them so happy."

CHAPTER 13

That evening, they decided to go out and celebrate. Dionne found Lynne and invited her and Dan to join them at Scottos, the 'in' local Italian restaurant. Harry and Dan caused a bit of a sensation when they arrived, but after a few photos with the owner, they were left alone. The restaurant was buzzing, the food was fantastic, and pretty soon the four of them were relaxed and having fun. Dionne noticed a few strange looks between Harry and Dan during dinner, as if there was some sort of private joke, but decided not to comment.

Suddenly Dan stood, scraping his chair back. He dropped to one knee beside Lynne, and held out a small box in front of her.

"Lynne, I love you with all my heart, would you marry me?"

The entire restaurant fell silent, waiting as one for her reply. Dionne held her breath.

Lynne took Dan's hand in hers and simply replied, "Yes." The place erupted in applause and cheers. Rather shakily, Dan slid the ring onto Lynne's slender finger, and blew out a held breath. The two of them grinned goofily at each other before Dan acknowledged their audience with a graceful bow. He sat back down in his chair, and grasped Lynne's hand to stare at the ring he had placed there.

Harry called the waiter and ordered a bottle of champagne to toast the happy couple, while Dionne admired the ring.

"It's so beautiful, did you choose it by yourself?" Dionne asked Dan. He grinned and puffed up proudly.

"All by myself," he bragged, pleased with himself. The ring looked as perfect on Lynne's finger as he had imagined when he chose it.

"Way to go Dan," said Harry, clapping him on the back, "and congratulations," as he stood to kiss Lynne. They toasted the happy couple with glasses of Cristal.

"Any idea where or how you want to get married?" asked Dionne.

"Not yet, but I'm sure it won't take us long to decide, probably easier to do it in the uk, but we have plenty of time to discuss what we want," replied Lynne, still grinning.

Harry smiled at Dionne, pleased to see her so happy for her friend.

'It's like my normal Di is back in town. Wonder if I'll ever get to put my ring on her finger.' He thought, looking wistfully at Lynne's new ring.

Later on, back home, Harry and Dionne sat in bed discussing the evening.

"Did you know he was gonna propose tonight?" She asked.

"Of course. I did check with you earlier if you thought she'd say yes if you remember," he replied, wrapping his arm round Dionne to pull her closer. He had missed sleeping next to her this past week. He liked wrapping around her little warm body and listening to her breathing as he fell asleep.

"I missed you this last week. I hate sleeping alone now," he admitted suddenly.

"Me too. This is nice," she replied, snuggling in deeper.

"You asked me if I pityfucked you, you don't honestly think that do you?" It had been eating at him since she had said it.

"No, I was just......oh I don't know, angry, upset, feeling insecure I suppose."

"I love you totally Di, never feel insecure about my feelings for you."

"I told you once how aware I am of the age gap. I still am sometimes. You might want the whole marriage and babies thing for all I know, and I can't give you that." She admitted. Harry could hear the sadness in her voice.

"I don't know if I want that or not. All I know is that I want to be with you. If that means I don't become a father, well you don't miss what you never had do you?"

"Spose not."

Harry rolled onto his back. "What was the reason you and John never had children?"

"Unexplained infertility. We both had tests done, but never got a definitive answer. Just not meant to be I guess," she replied, the sadness in her voice even more evident.

"You know you haven't had a period all the time we've been together," said Harry. He didn't know much about these things, but knew from biology class that women tended to have one every month.

"Mine have always been erratic, it may well be the start of the menopause or something," she replied.

'Oh great, hot flushes and vaginal dryness to look forward to, super' she thought.

"I'm probably due one soon, I feel fat and my breasts are a bit tender."

Harry grunted in reply. In truth he was a bit pleased. He had never had a girlfriend as such, so dealing with the basic female biology was new to him, reserved for normal men with normal girlfriends or wives. Now he had a girlfriend. The thought thrilled him.

"We have company this weekend, the guys who helped me out are coming to stay for a bit of R and R, and to share out the spoils." She told Harry.

"Ok, what spoils are they?"

"A yacht, house, art collection, that kind of thing."

"What, James' stuff?"

"Yes. I'll probably have his art collection. It's not bad." Said Dionne sleepily.

"Why would you want anything of that fuckers?" Said Harry, taking Dionne by surprise. She lay there thinking about it, it hadn't occurred to her before that she wouldn't want to be reminded of him.

"It's not the arts fault," was all she could come up with.

"Still," he replied, wondering about the Mayfair house, which would be a good rental investment. He decided not to make a fuss or push the issue in case he got the opportunity to buy it cheap.

He heard her breathing even out, so he wrapped himself around her and went to sleep.

Dionne was still sleeping when he left for the studio the next morning.

'Probably fried from the week she just had' he thought.

Harry padded around quietly so as not to wake her. He shaved and dressed quickly, and left the bedroom silently. His new bodyguard was waiting for him downstairs to accompany him to work.

She finally awoke at ten, the latest she had slept in for many years. She threw on some shorts and a vest and went to find Lynne, cross with herself for missing such a momentous latte o'clock. She found Lynne in the gym, just finishing a session with her personal trainer.

"Latte by the pool?" Dionne called out.

"Nearly done, five minutes yeah?" Puffed Lynne. Her LA trainer was a wiry, super fit young woman with a sadistic streak who seemed to think that if she didn't turn her punters purple, she was somehow not doing her job.

Dionne wandered down to the kitchen to ask for their coffees and something to eat. She was starving. Chef had been making Danish pastries for the security team, so she nabbed one of those to scoff while she was waiting for her breakfast.

'No wonder I'm putting on weight' she thought guiltily.

Back beside the pool, Lynne was waiting. They sipped their coffees while Lynne gushed about how happy she was, and what they had discussed wedding wise. They both quite fancied getting married in the rather pretty village church in Upper Slaughter, and having the reception in the ballroom of the house. Dionne clapped her hands together.

"Sounds so romantic, we can make the ballroom look beautiful. When do you want to do it?" She asked.

"I thought May, because the grounds are so gorgeous that time of year," replied Lynne, with a dreamy smile on her face as she thought of the acres of billowing cherry blossom.

"What does Dan want?"

"He just said as soon as possible, so I think May is fine with him."

"You got some organising to do to pull it off that quick."

"I know, but it's so exciting, I can't wait," said Lynne, her eyes shining with joy.

Dionne told her friend about the guests arriving the next day which made Lynne groan.

"I think I might fly to England and start the preparations, you know, see if I can book the church and stuff. I don't fancy having to be the one to tell old Diwarni the bad news." She laughed.

"Shall I get you a jet for when Dan finishes work today? Then he can go with you." Dionne offered.

"Great, I'll let him know," said Lynne, pulling out her phone to text Dan.

Dionne spent the rest of the day briefing the household staff about the plans for the weekend. She organised flights and connecting helicopters for Lynne and Dan, before checking all the indices for untoward consequences. Harry found her fast asleep at her keyboard, her head rested on her folded arms. He gently shook her shoulder.

"Hey baby, you were out for the count," he chuckled as she raised sleepy blue eyes.

She yawned. "Consequence of a week of no sleep. I'm crashing a bit now. Early night tonight I think."

They ate early, outside on the terrace, chatting about Lynne's ideas for the wedding, which Harry thought sounded great.

"What time are our guests arriving tomorrow?" He asked.

"About midday. I thought we would have lunch on the terrace, deal with business, then tennis, croquet and pool volleyball. Four of them are bringing partners, so I'll need you to help me host if that's ok."

Harry perked up considerably. It wouldn't just be five men fawning over Dionne this time. He began to quite look forward to it.

"No problem, I can look after wives when you talk shop." He gave her his best knicker dropping smile, which made her laugh.

"Now is there anything of James' that you want? I thought about saying no to his art collection, but there really is some superb pieces. I think Darren wants that yacht we went on in Barbados, but there's still his house." She looked expectantly at Harry.

"How much is his house going to be?" Asked Harry a bit sheepishly.

"Five mill, it's worth about ten on the open market, but he sold it to the sheik for cash in desperation that day, our deal is that we divvy these things up at cost."

"If you think it's a good investment for me as a rental property, then yes, I'd like it." He muttered, a bit embarrassed at having been pissy about her having the art collection.

"Okey doke. I'll have to see if Diwarni wants to keep it, but if not, I'll pick it up for you," she said kindly.

They went to bed almost straight after dinner, and made love slowly, gently caressing each other until they each found their release. Dionne fell asleep almost immediately. Harry switched the telly on, and flicked through the channels aimlessly. He watched Dionne sleep, noticing the peaceful look on her beautiful face.

'Im jealous of Dan. There, I've admitted it. I want to get married, make her Mrs Cooper. I want her sleeping beside me like this forever. I want to make her mine.'

Thinking those thoughts, he switched off the TV and wrapped himself around her in his favourite sleeping position.

The next morning they both woke early and treated themselves to a morning orgasm each before showering and dressing. After breakfast, Dionne checked all the guest bedrooms to make sure that everything was perfect, while Harry checked over the pool and tennis courts. The house smelt fabulous thanks to ornate flower displays in all the rooms.

As their guests arrived, Dionne introduced everyone to Harry. She knew the three wives well, only Darren's date had to be introduced.

"Dionne, Harry, this is Poppy, my girlfriend," said Darren, proudly.

"Poppy, how nice to meet you, we didn't get introduced at the crystal ball," said Dionne.

Poppy smiled widely, excited that Dionne had recognised her. The private jet had been so fantastic, and now staying at this mansion was just beyond her expectations. She was a bit intimidated by it all.

"Thank you. I don't remember seeing you at the ball, but I got introduced to so many of Darren's friends that night, it became a bit of a blur." She giggled, "your house is beyond beautiful."

"Thank you," smiled Dionne, instantly warming to her.

They served a sumptuous lunch on the terrace, their guests enjoying a cold salmon salad, rack of lamb and summer pudding to finish. Harry chose the various wines to accompany their lunch from the large, well stocked cellar underneath the house.

The atmosphere was convivial and the conversation flowed. It was decided that after lunch, Harry would organise a game of croquet while the men and Dionne had their meeting. Dionne glanced over at Harry, who had his best smile and charm switched on. The four women were delighted with the arrangement, clearly pleased at being escorted by a gorgeous film star for the afternoon. At that moment, she loved him even more.

The five men sat around the large dining table, as they had done two weeks previously. Dionne opened the meeting.

"Thank you all for everything you did. We will begin by disclosing all gains and losses. If you would exclude James' personal assets from your balance, as per our agreement, it would be helpful." She said to Sheik Diwarni. She began with Darren.

"Up seven hundred and forty eight million."

"Good, George?"

"One point three billion." Replied Mr Boros, smirking. She looked at Alexander.

"One point seven billion. Well done Di," he said.

"Sultan?" Asked Dionne.

"Three point one billion."

All eyes rested on the Sheik. "Two point nine five billion."

Dionne smiled widely. "Well I'm up three point seven billion, so I would suggest this was a successful heist in more ways than one. Now all we have left to discuss are Mr Rankin's personal losses."

George spoke up. "We have discussed this already. The sheik has been adequately recompensed by us all for the art, house and boat of Mr Rankin. We would like you to have them as restitution for the wrong that was done." The men all nodded in agreement.

"Aw guys, that's so kind," was all Dionne could manage, as she looked round the table at the men who had stepped up to help her.

"Being able to watch how you operate at such close quarters was worth a few million. Like a masterclass in strategy," said Darren.

"A toast," proposed Alexander,"to the chess player, may we never come up against you."

"Salut."

They sat for a further half hour discussing the finer points of some of the trades and strategies that Dionne had put together, all expressing their admiration that the project had been so swift and successful.

After concluding the meeting, they all returned to the terrace to find Alexander's wife, Simone, and Poppy playing tennis. Harry was charming a mesmerised Lorena Boros and Sultana Fazani with Hollywood gossip. Dionne kissed him gratefully on the cheek, and sat down next to Lorena while Harry went off to watch the tennis. The two women were good friends, having known each other for around fifteen years. Lorena smiled indulgently at Dionne.

"You did well last week, but have you thought about what it cost you?" She said.

Dionne blinked. "In what way do you mean?"

Lorena sighed, "Harry. He's quite the catch, but I'm worried he is scared of what you are now that you have revealed yourself to him. How many men want such a powerful woman?"

Dionne's stomach sank. Maybe Lorena was right. She knew Harry loved her, wanted to be with her, but he hadn't proposed.

'Maybe it's just too soon' she thought.

"You may be right Lorena, but the thing is, I can't just wish it all away. Harry has to know the truth, otherwise I would be being unfair if I hid aspects of myself." She explained.

"That's true, but I'm sure that every time he fantasises about you being Mrs Cooper, a little voice in his head shouts 'Golddigger'," said Lorena, looking concerned. She went on, "I'll talk to him, see if I'm right, and try and put his mind at rest."

"Thank you Lorena, that would help. He's well off in his own right, but he has said a few times that he finds my wealth a bit overwhelming at times."

"Well I've been a billionaire's wife for forty years now, so I'm pretty well qualified in the pluses and minuses," laughed Lorena, patting Dionne's hand affectionately.

The dinner that evening was spectacular. Dionne's chefs had truly surpassed themselves in laying on a banquet which nodded towards middle eastern cuisine without being a slavish copy. Dionne was seated between Darren and Alexander. She listened as Darren waxed lyrical about how lovely Poppy was. As Dionne had herself warmed to the beautiful model, she was pleasantly surprised to discover that Poppy had achieved a first in chemistry at Oxford. Darren explained that she was earning more as a model than she would as a scientist. Her plan was to model for a few more years, then try and find a research position in a pharmaceutical company.

"She's the one isn't she?" Dionne probed. Darren flushed pink, and cleared his throat.

"Yes, I think she is. She struggles with the inequality of our positions though," he admitted, shifting uncomfortably.

"In what way?" Said Dionne, frowning slightly.

"She likes to achieve through her own merit, and I think she fears I will negate the need for her to do that. Lets face it, she wouldn't need to work or earn if she married me, and for a clever woman, that's a problem."

"Could the two of you not build together like John and I did? There was no senior partner in our marriage."

"Easier when you are both young. I'm older, established, it's more complicated." Confided Darren.

Meanwhile, Harry was having a similar conversation with Lorena at the other end of the table.

"You need to get a ring on her finger Harry," said Lorena. "Don't let all this cloud your opinion, even billionaires are human beings."

"I'd love to, but this little voice in my head whispers gold digger at me. Plus I feel like a total thicko around her at times." He admitted, glad to have found someone to discuss it with.

"My husband feels like that around her too at times, and he's no slouch in the brain cell department I can tell you."

"Really? I find that hard to believe. I just worry she would be happier with someone more like her, like John was." Harry said.

"John wasn't clever like her. Where did you get that idea? He was a people person, charming, fun and easy to get along with. Dionne made all the money." Lorena revealed.

Harry's mind reeled at the revelation. "You're sure about that?"

"Absolutely. Very few people are as intellectually gifted as Dionne, it doesn't mean she can't relate to others in a normal way though. Writing her off as too clever for you is a bit unfair, she is clearly in love with you, especially the way she fought to protect your career from her own actions this past week."

Harry looked quizzical "what do you mean?"

"James knew she invested heavily in your studio, so when she screwed James over, they had to prevent him hiding money in universal. She didn't want to have to liquidate the company you work for" Lorena explained.

"How did she do that?" He asked, his mind working overtime to try and understand.

"She sent Darren to head him off at the pass. Darren persuaded him to split his money between two investments, and the six of them forced his bankruptcy that way. It was very clever."

"Sounds it," agreed Harry.

"I can see the way you look at her, you appear so proud of her. It's lovely being with an intelligent person, trust me," said Lorena, smiling at Harry, "and I bet she can't keep her hands off of such a gorgeous hunk of man like you. If I was thirty years younger, I'd eat you alive young man." She winked, which made Harry laugh.

"Down girl!" He chided, "don't want your husband getting jealous now do we?"

The evening was a great success, the conversation flowed freely, as did the champagne. At one in the morning, the guests all headed up to bed. Harry unzipped Dionne's dress before stripping off and sliding under the covers. She snuggled into his arms.·

"Thank you for making today such a success, I know you don't know these people well, but you were fantastic." She said, kissing his chest.

190

"They're all nice people, I like meeting your friends. Lorena's a real blast."

"She's great. What were the two of you whispering about at the table?"

"She told me that billionaires are normal people too, and I shouldn't be intimidated by your wealth." Harry had decided to be candid.

"Are you?"

Harry sucked in a deep breath. "Truthfully? Yes, sometimes. I'm also intimidated by your brain. I wonder sometimes why you want me when I'm not clever."

"You looked in a mirror lately Mr genetically perfect? You're gorgeous, rich and great company. You're knowledgable about wine, charming, and half the females in the western world would like to see your dick. Do I need to carry on?"

Harry laughed and tugged her closer. "You really have a way with words Di."

"I'd like to think I'm a bit more desirable than just a brain on legs," she huffed.

"Are you mad? You are the sexiest woman I have ever met, I think we proved that one beyond all doubt. You know I lust after you. I would have thought you'd be offended if I only loved your body, and not your amazing mind."

"Well, yes, just don't let it intimidate you. I still have insecurities too, as you already know. Money doesn't buy everything." She said, before teasing his nipple with her tongue. He slid his hand down her body to stroke between her legs. Feeling her arousal, he rolled her onto her back before turning his attention to her breasts.

"You know what I loved about today?" He murmured against her nipple.

"What?"

"I got so fucking horny watching all those men worshipping you, knowing I'm the only one that gets to do this."

She giggled. "And those women staring at your beautiful smile, knowing that only I get to make you scream."

He nudged his cock inside her, moving slowly, gliding in and out at a gentle pace, savouring her. She caressed his shoulders and muscular chest, the feel of his silky, warm skin turning her on. Keeping a slow rhythm, he reached between them to rub tiny circles on her clit. He felt her begin to quiver and ripple around him, until she came, her orgasm washing over her in waves, causing her to arch off the bed. As her orgasm subsided, Harry let himself come, his cock jerking inside her. He stayed inside her, wrapping his arms around her to hold her tightly, not wanting to break their connection.

"You are a beautiful man," whispered Dionne,"and I love you."

"I love you too baby, more than you would ever know," he replied.

The following day they all had breakfast in the grand dining room. The chefs had laid out a wonderful spread ranging from platters of fruit, pastries and muffins through to full English in all it's combinations. Harry arranged with Alexander, Simone and Poppy to play a game of mixed doubles. Everyone else planned to relax by the pool.

"Are you genuinely a chess player Di?" Darren asked.

"Yes, I play," she replied.

"How about a game on the terrace?" Challenged Darren.

Dionne smirked. "Sure, I'll get the butler to set it up."

After the tennis, Harry wandered back to the terrace to find an audience gathered around Dionne and Darren.

"Checkmate."

"How in gods name did you do that? Bloody glad we're not playing for money you annoying woman," whined Darren, to peals of laughter from their audience.

"Third time lucky Darren?" Challenged Dionne, looking pleased with herself.

"No, I think I've been humiliated enough. Anyone else want to try and play her?" Darren said to the surrounding men, who all sheepishly shook their heads.

Poppy called out "I'll have a go. I've played before." She swapped places with Darren, who was relieved to be off the hook. He fancied himself as quite the chess player, so Dionne's quick demolition of his game twice had been a bit galling.

While the girls played chess, Lorena found Harry and asked him to escort her on a tour of the grounds. She hooked her arm through his, and they set off.

"Did you talk to Di last night?" Inquired Lorena.

"A bit. I admitted that I found her a little intimidating."

"And?"

"She just said that money can't buy everything, so I suppose she means I should look past it." He replied.

Lorena sighed. "What you must remember is that for these people, it's actually not about the money. Once you hit about half a billion, you can afford what you want for a lifetime. For my husband, Dionne and the others, it's about winning, being on the correct side of a bet. The billions are just their measure of success, nothing more."

Harry frowned at her, "so Dionne does it for the hell of it?"

"Almost. It's a game, in the same way that they are playing chess right now for the fun of it, she plays financial chess. The wealth is just a by product. They see money in a different way than we do." She went on, "Dionne and Lynne have a normal friendship. Lynne is no Einstein, she's a bloody liability at times, and yet they have a sisterly relationship that has lasted thirty years. Dionne gives Lynne free access to whatever money she wants because the money isn't important to her, but Lynne is. Do you get what I'm telling you?"

"I think so," said Harry, pondering it over in his mind.

"What I'm telling you is to concentrate on your feelings for each other, and your compatibility, and really don't worry about her bank balance, because I doubt that she gives yours a second thought."

"I love her," admitted Harry.

"I can tell, and she is in love with you too. So tell me, do I need to buy a hat?" Pressed Lorena, giving Harry such a hopeful smile that it made him laugh.

"I do hope so, I'll try and find the right moment."

They made their way back to the terrace. Nobody noticed them approach due to the exciting game of chess that had captured everyone's attention. Harry looked at the board in surprise, noting that Poppy appeared to be giving Dionne a run for her money. Watching Dionne, he could almost see her intense concentration, and the possible permutations flashing through her mind. She was totally calm, and appeared not to notice the people around her.

It took a further six moves each for Dionne to declare a checkmate. It had been pretty close though.

"Darren, you need to teach Poppy finance, she has the most incredible, strategic brain," said Dionne, shaking hands with Poppy.

"I'd love to learn to do what all of you do," admitted Poppy.

Darren gazed at her with what could only be described as a mixture of love, lust and pride. "If you want to learn finance, just say the word

194

honey, and I'll sort you a job."

She beamed at him in response, delighted at Dionne's compliment, and pleased that she had given a good game.

CHAPTER 14

After lunch on the terrace, limousines arrived to pick up their guests and deliver them to LAX. After they had all left, Harry and Dionne flopped down in the living room and ordered coffees.

"I think that constituted a great success," said Harry.

"Definitely. They all loved you. Lorena can't get enough of you, and the Sultana couldn't take her eyes off you."

"Just a pretty face baby, anyway, they were all here for you. Dare I ask about the Mayfair house and art?"

"The guys all paid the Sheik between them and gave me the house, art and yacht as my restitution." Dionne looked tentative as Harry spat his coffee out.

"You are joking?" He was incredulous.

"They all made shitloads out of this, a few million each didn't even dent their profits."

"Jeez, it's a different world around you. So you have a yacht now?"

"Yep. Apparently it's moored in St Lucia at the moment. The Sheik gave me all the paperwork and keys yesterday."

"Wow, sorts out a honeymoon for Lynne and Dan maybe?" Suggested Harry.

"What a lovely idea, I'll give her a call and run it past her, they won't be in the air just yet," said Dionne, checking her watch.

She picked up the phone and dialled Lynne. Harry couldn't follow the one sided conversation, but it appeared that Dan was being consulted too. Dionne ended the call.

"Both delighted, plus, they were able to persuade the vicar to fit them in to marry on the 12th of May, just after Dan finishes filming. They are back here early hours of tomorrow, then Lynne's going back the week after next to get everything organised. I might fly to St Lucia next week to check out the yacht, see if it needs any work doing, and clear out any personal items in there." Dionne said excitedly. She noticed that Harry looked pensive.

"What's up?" She asked.

Harry took a deep breath while he tried to find the words. "I'm jealous of Dan," he admitted.

Dionne looked horrified. "You fancy Lynne?" She asked, incredulous.

"No! Don't be daft, no I'm jealous of him being married to the woman he loves."

'That's it, it's out' he thought.

"You want to be married?" Asked Dionne.

"Yes" said Harry in a small voice, feeling needy.

"To me? Or is it more an abstract 'being married' you want?"

"You," said Harry in an even smaller voice, looking down at his nails.

"Is this a proposal?" Dionne was giving nothing away.

"Sort of I spose." Harry couldn't look at her.

'What if she says no?' He thought.

"Generally the man asks while on bended knee."

Harry looked up at her to see her beaming smile.

'Fuck it, I'm gonna do it'

He put his coffee down, and kneeled in front of her. He grasped her hand and nervously met her gaze.

"I love you Di, will you marry me?"

She looked deep into his eyes, "yes, I'd love to."

'Did she really just say yes? Oh my god, she said yes'

Harry grabbed her and hugged her, lifting her off the ground. "I can't believe it, you said yes! I am the happiest man alive," he yelled, swinging her round excitedly. He set her down and kissed her, a deep loving kiss, trying to communicate the feelings he couldn't find the words for.

She broke away, breathless, "I didn't think you'd ever ask. I was even contemplating getting Dan to push you," she admitted.

Harry laughed, "Dan already knew I wanted to ask you. I went with him to get Lynne's ring. Erm, I picked one out for you, you can change it if you don't like it though, I won't be offended." Suddenly he was nervous. He ran upstairs to retrieve the box hidden in his sock drawer, and brought it back downstairs. Handing it to Dionne, he held his breath.

She opened it to reveal the huge oval diamond in the simple, elegant platinum setting. It was so perfect it took her breath away.

"It's beautiful, perfect, I love it, thank you." She said, letting him slide it onto her finger.

Harry let out the breath he had been holding.

"When I chose this, I tried to imagine how it would look on this finger. I actually can't believe I'm really looking at it now, and it's better than I ever dreamt." He said, staring at her hand.

Dionne text Lynne

Harry proposed. Said yes.

"She'll be shaking you awake at four in the morning to get the lowdown," laughed Harry. "Now you just have to decide where and when."

"What would you prefer?" Dionne asked, anxious to avoid making all the decisions.

"Personally I'd like to go to Vegas tomorrow and tie the knot, but I'm sure you would rather do it properly." Grinned Harry.

"So sooner rather than later?"

"Suits me. I really don't mind where or when. Register office or church, whatever makes you happy."

"You make me happy. I'll give it some thought. Probably better to wait till your jobs finished in three months time," said Dionne. She figured it would be awkward for Harry to leave LA until he finished filming.

"You're going to be Mrs Cooper. The smartest, cleverest, most beautiful woman in the world is gonna be my wife. That's insane," mused Harry.

"Dionne Cooper. Sounds great. I'm going to practice my new signature tomorrow."

Harry pulled out his phone and text Lorena

mission accomplished. Buy a hat :D

He showed the text to Dionne, which made her giggle.

They spent the rest of the evening planning, grinning and just being in love.

That night, Dionne undressed Harry, stroking his dick, "mine," she said.

He slid her knickers down and caressed between her legs, "mine."

They made love starting slowly, arousing each other, savouring the moment, before becoming more passionate. Harry nipped and licked Dionne's body before sliding inside her to bring her to a shattering climax. He watched her come apart beneath him, marvelling at how far they had come in just a few months. The years of being afraid of sex seemed like another lifetime ago.

She opened her eyes to watch him come, his beautiful face becoming even more handsome as his brow furrowed in concentration. He gripped her tightly, pressing their bodies together as he came.

Afterwards, he wrapped around her and held her tight as they fell asleep.

They both woke early, and after making love, shared a shower. Harry didn't have to be on set till eight, so they had time to eat a leisurely breakfast on the terrace before Harry's bodyguard was showing up to escort him to work.

He decided to broach a subject that had been bothering him. "Do you want me to sign a prenup before the wedding?"

"No." Dionne replied immediately. "I don't think we need one do you?"

"No, but it would dispel any worries about gold digging once and for all," said Harry, a bit puzzled.

"A better way to do that is if I drop a couple of billion in your current account. If you're only with me for money, I doubt if you'd hang around to get married."

"You don't need to do that." Laughed Harry.

"I think it's a great idea actually, I might do it this morning, see if you come home tonight." She laughed at the look of horror on his face.

'Cheaper than a divorce baby' she thought.

The news of their engagement was spreading fast thanks to Lorena, who called Dionne to squeal down the phone, and find out the details of Harrys proposal.

"I'm so pleased for you Di," she gushed, "he's such a catch, and the two of you together are just perfect."

"I know, he really is gorgeous, I feel really lucky. Thank you for pushing him, I really owe you for that."

"Nonsense, he loves you, and he would have figured it all out, I just speeded things up. Now, any decisions yet about the wedding?"

"Not yet, although I was considering Barbados. Lynne got back last night from booking hers, so I'll talk to her before I make a decision. She booked the church at Upper Slaughter for May the twelfth."

"Mad isn't it that you both found husbands at the same time, and they are best friends too. Funny how life pans out isn't it? Now if you were to both have babies at the same time, well, that would be fabulous." Lorena said, her voice rather wistful. Lorena had five children, and babies were her most favourite thing in the world.

"I know Lynne and Dan are trying, but I can't have children, so we might have to make do with being godparents instead." Dionne tried not to sound sad.

"Well, if its meant to be, it'll happen," said Lorena, " now, can you take a photo of the ring and send it to me, I want to spend my day in a wistful, romantic haze."

"Will do, and thank you."

Dionne photographed her ring, and sent it over to Lorena as promised. She sat on the terrace, in the sunshine, looking at her new ring.

'Does life really get any better than this?'

Lynne surfaced at around eleven, bringing coffees for a rather late latte o'clock. She examined Dionne's ring, declared it 'adorable', and proceeded to talk ten to the dozen about booking the church.

"Why don't we make it a double wedding?" Suggested Lynne.

Dionne thought about it. "Hmm, it's an idea, but I don't want to steal your thunder. I think I'd rather you have your big day, then I'll have mine."

"Don't you think timings will be awkward if I get married on the twelfth and go on honeymoon, and you want to get married in June?" Lynne pointed out.

"Hmm, good point. Shall we all discuss it tonight over dinner? Get the boy's take on the idea?" Suggested Dionne.

"Good idea, now tell me about this yacht. Do you want me to come to St Lucia with you tomorrow to help?" Lynne asked hopefully. She always enjoyed a decorating project.

"As long as Dan doesn't mind, that would be great. I have no idea if James' stuff is still onboard or not, and I haven't seen the accommodation on there. The deck is pretty fantastic, and I'm sure James spared no expense inside. We can fly down tomorrow morning."

"Great, I'll pack us a bag each," said Lynne excitedly. She disappeared off into the house. Dionne followed her in to book a jet, and call her bank.

That evening, they all had dinner together on the terrace, and discussed wedding plans. Much to Dionne's surprise, both men thought a double wedding was a great idea. Dan promised to call the vicar the following day to find out if it would be possible.

Lynne was excited about her plans for the ballroom at the house. She had spoken to some party planning companies, and was confident a fairy tale wedding could be organised in the timeframe.

"That leaves dresses, bridesmaids, flowers and a guest list to sort out," she said, "spoke to Sarah at McQueen about a dress, it's doable. Dan has two nieces who would love to be bridesmaids, the florist who does our normal flowers said she would do the bridal stuff, so that just leaves guests. Dan's mum is working on her family list already, just friends to go." Lynne didn't have any family apart from an ageing great aunt who she hadn't seen for thirty years.

"Do you have any nieces or nephews?" Dionne asked Harry.

"Yes, both my older brothers have families. Two nieces, and one nephew in total." He replied.

Lynne clapped her hands together. "Perfect. The church can hold only three hundred at a squeeze though. Dan has quite a large family, so we have to keep within those numbers."

The following day they flew down to St Lucia. Driving towards the marina, Dionne pointed out 'The Pied Piper' to Lynne.

"Wow! Jesus Christ Di, that sure is some compensation. I didn't think it would be as big as that," gasped Lynne.

The security team went aboard to do a sweep while Dionne spoke to the harbour master, and settled the mooring fees. As soon as Craig gave them the all clear, they went on board.

Starting off in the accommodation, Dionne was pleasantly surprised that the decor was similar to her Barbados home. The main drawing room had large cream leather seating built in, and a huge bar set along one wall.

"So far so good," said Lynne, impressed. They explored the bedrooms and bathrooms. There were five good bedrooms, each with a stylish ensuite, with nothing needing replacing. Dionne noticed that James' things were still in the master bedroom, and needed to be cleared out. She nosed through the closets, and decided to donate all the clothes to charity shops on the island.

There didn't seem to be anything else of interest, until she came upon a door at the back of the dressing room. It was reminiscent of her jewellery room door at home, and immediately piqued her curiosity. She called Lynne to come and see.

The door was locked, so Dionne went through all the keys the Sheik had given her until the lock clicked open. She pushed the door, and they crept in. Dionne fumbled for a light switch as the room was pitch dark. The light clicked on, illuminating a scene which made Dionne's hand fly in front of her mouth, and Lynne to cry out "holy fuck."

The first thing Dionne noticed was the enormous pale blue cot. It was tucked against a wall, and had a pretty, blue patchwork quilt on it. They ventured further into the room, taking it all in. Lynne lifted the lid of a large toy box that had pictures of soldiers painted on the outside. Inside she found a selection of children's toys. Teddy bears, toy cars and Lego being the most popular. There was a TV set on a cupboard which housed DVDs, and a small desk with a laptop on it. Dionne opened the wardrobe, to be confronted by a selection of giant babygros, and packs of adult diapers.

"Di, look at this," said Lynne, looking in the last cupboard. Inside was a collection of canes, whips and floggers. Dionne blanched.

"He really was one sick puppy," said Dionne, staring at the canes. She pulled out her mobile, and text Harry.

call me ASAP, urgent

Meanwhile, Lynne had found a huge changing mat tucked behind the sofa. She began to giggle.

Dionne switched on the laptop. She clicked on history, seeing straight away that it had been used mainly to visit adult baby forums.

"Can you believe what you're seeing?" Dionne said, picking up an oversized dummy rather gingerly.

Lynne snorted, trying not to give in to the laughter that was bubbling up. She pulled one of the enormous babygros from the wardrobe, and held it up. Seeing the blue bunnies appliquéd onto the chest, she collapsed into helpless laughter, swiftly followed by Dionne.

"We shouldn't laugh, the poor mans dead, and your old man is probably gonna want the cot," gasped Lynne, before they both howled with laughter again.

"And the Lego," Dionne managed to say before they both dissolved again.

Meanwhile, Harry spotted Dionne's text after finishing a take. He called her straightaway. "Hey baby, what's up?" He could hear laughter in the background that sounded suspiciously like Lynne's. Dionne motioned to Lynne to shut up, which caused Lynne to run from the room and close the door, unable to control herself.

"Harry, you are never in a million years gonna guess what we found."

"Go on."

"A fully fitted adult nursery."

"You having me on?"

"No, there really is one. Let me get a lock on the boats wifi, and I'll FaceTime you. Call you back in a mo."

Dionne found the study, and after rifling through some drawers, found the wifi password. She called Harry back using the FaceTime application. She showed him around the nursery, laughing when he went 'ew' at the adult diapers. He snickered at the babygros, and commented 'dirty bastard' at the whip and cane collection. When she had shown him all round the room, she turned the phone to face him.

"Didn't expect that at all. Must have been quite a shock," said Harry.

"Definitely. The rest of the boat is really nicely done. We just have to get rid of his stuff, and get it cleaned," said Dionne, not wanting to ask Harry if he wanted to keep anything.

"Erm."

"Yes?" She could see him blush.

"Keep the cot and stuff eh? Not the clothes or nappies, and chuck out the whips and chains yeah?"

"Sure." She wasn't going to make a big deal of it. *'Each to their own'* she thought.

"Listen, I gotta go baby, I'm being called. You and Lynne have a good time there, and I'll speak to you later," said Harry, blowing her a kiss.

"Bye, love you," she replied, sending a thrill through him.

She went off to find Lynne, who was in the kitchen marshalling a cleaning crew to do a deep clean of the whole boat. Dionne found two of their security guards to help her clear out the master bedroom.

They checked all the pockets of the suits before loading them into bags for the charity shop. Craig was quite disappointed that none of the designer suits were his size. Dionne slung all the whips into black bags, along with the other items in the room that Harry didn't want. She then locked the door, and concentrated on the study.

Dionne went through all the contents of the drawers carefully. Most of it was rubbish, flyers, old paperwork and receipts. All she kept were items related directly to the boat. She switched on his computer and checked through it, finding only market data and work stuff. She looked carefully around the room. There was still a key on the ring that she hadn't found a use for, so she figured he must have had a safe.

She searched the study inch by inch, until she came to a bookshelf. She checked behind the books and found the safe. Unlocking it with the final key, she pulled out the contents and laid them on the desk. She found papers relating to the boats purchase, which she replaced in the safe. She put a couple of memory sticks to one side, and threw away a load of old chequebooks and bank statements. At the bottom of the pile was a large flat box. Opening it, she found dozens of photographs of young men and women in various stages of torture. Horrified, she called Lynne in.

Lynne sifted through the photos, whistling through her teeth. "Some of these look underage to me. I think we need to burn these, rather than just chucking them."

"Those poor kids. Some of them look terrified," said Dionne, "all that feeling bad about what we did to him has evaporated, I think we did the world a favour seeing these."

She replaced the photos, closed the box and called Craig in. Handing him the box and the chequebooks, she asked him to go ashore and burn them. She plugged the first memory stick into the computer, finding that it contained only video files. Taking a deep breath, she opened the first one. The film began rather hazy, until James could be seen adjusting the camera. A young girl was tied up on a bed, looking terrified as James beat her with a cane. Dionne quickly closed the file. Each of the files contained similar imagery.

She checked through the second stick, to find every file showed similar scenes of torture and depravity, although, primarily with young boys as opposed to girls.

The third and final stick contained image upon image of James in his nursery. Pictures of him in a babygro, in a nappy, with a dummy, the list went on. Dionne noticed that some of the images seemed to be taken in a different nursery than the one she had found on the boat. *'There must be another one at his house'* she thought.

She took the three memory sticks onto the deck, and threw them into the sea.

The big clear out took two days, including an enormous shopping trip to Miami for Lynne to buy new bedding and other household stuff. When they were satisfied that everything was organised and cleaned up, they headed back to LA.

They arrived back early evening, in time to share dinner with their fiancés. They showed Harry and Dan pictures of the yacht, making plans to spend the weekend there, and explore St Lucia a bit more. They agreed to fly down Friday night after work, taking some staff.

Dan had spoken to the vicar, who had agreed to do a double wedding on the twelfth, in exchange for a donation to the church roof fund.

Harry had spoken to his director and the studio. All his filming was being brought forward so that his part would be finished before the wedding, which freed him for the honeymoon. He had also spoken to Ralph about taking time off after the wedding, instructing him not to schedule any appearances for at least two months.

Dionne couldn't remember ever being this happy. Everything was falling into place. She caught Harrys eye and smiled as he beamed back at her.

The next day at latte o'clock, Lynne dropped a bit of a bombshell. "My period's late, only a few days, but definitely late."

"Might just be where you only came off the pill a month or so ago," pointed out Dionne.

"Yeah, maybe."

"I've not had one for about four months. Keep feeling like I'm due on though, all fat and uncomfortable," said Dionne.

Lynne sighed, "I might do a test, at least if it's a no, I won't get my hopes up."

"Good idea," agreed Dionne.

They spent the rest of latte o'clock discussing wedding dress styles, and colour schemes, deciding on cream for the bridesmaids and pageboy.

That afternoon Lynne tracked Dionne down in the library. "I bought some pregnancy tests," she said nervously. "I'm scared though, come and do this with me?"

Dutifully, Dionne followed her upstairs to her room, and sat on the bed. Lynne had bought a large selection of tests, and had piled them onto the bedside table. Dionne picked one up, and opened it to pull out the instructions. It was all pretty straightforward.

"Just wee on the end of the stick, and wait five minutes. Seems quite simple."

"You should do one too Di, I mean putting on weight, missing periods, and you were throwing up for a while," Lynne pointed out.

"More like menopause than pregnant," laughed Dionne, "its pointless, but if it makes you happy I'll do one too." She opened another box and went into Dan's bathroom. Doing the test, she mused *'pointless doing this, just be a disappointment, Harrys child, hmm, babies in the house. Nice dream Di, not gonna happen, don't be disappointed.'*

A few minutes later, they met back up in the bedroom, both clutching their tests. Dionne looked at her watch, "right, five minutes starts now." They sat side by side on the bed watching as both tests turned blue, while Dionne turned pale.

"Oh. My. God!" Screamed Lynne, "I knew it! I bloody knew it!" She danced around the bedroom in joy, as Dionne sat on the bed in shock. *'What the fuck?'*

"I need to do another test, this one might be faulty," muttered Dionne, in shock.

Three tests later, the two of them were still sitting on the bed when Dan arrived home.

"Dan! Tests positive! You're gonna be a daddy!" Lynne yelled. Dan hugged her tight, a huge beaming smile on his face.

"The best news ever babe. You're gonna be a Momma," he said, "can I see the test? I want to make sure this is real, I'm really gonna be a Dad." Lynne showed him the two test sticks she had done. It was at this point that he noticed Dionne sitting on the bed, silent, clutching three sticks.

"You alright Di?" He asked.

"She's pregnant too. Isn't that brilliant?" Trilled Lynne.

"Have you told Harry yet? He's gonna be stoked."

"No, he's not home yet. Do you really think he'll be happy? This is a bit of a shock to say the least." Dionne replied, looking dazed.

Dan looked at her as if she was mad, "he will be totally over the moon, trust me." He turned back to Lynne, "when do we get to do the scan babe? I want to see what's going on in there," he said, patting her tummy.

"I'll call the doctor and find out," said Lynne, reaching for her phone.

Harry had had a good day. Lots of one take scenes, an invite to the Oscars, and various parties, and was now heading home early to his woman. He sat in the back of the Bentley daydreaming about his wedding day. The knowledge that Dionne was happy to become Mrs Cooper gave him a thrill. He had been convinced she wouldn't want to change her name. Idly, he wondered if she had been practising her new signature like a teenage girl. The car pulled up outside the mansion, and as always, he thanked the gods for his good fortune. The door swung open, Connor there to usher him inside, and take his briefcase.

"The others are waiting for you in the drawing room sir," announced Connor. Puzzled, Harry strode over to the doorway and walked in. He noticed Dionne looked pale, and Dan and Lynne were both beaming.

"Hi, is everything alright?" Harry frowned.

"I have something to tell you," said Dionne, looking so pensive that his stomach fell into his boots. "You know I said I couldn't have children?"

"Of course," replied Harry, perplexed.

"I did a pregnancy test this afternoon."

"And?"

"I'm pregnant. I don't know how it happened, but it has," said Dionne, cringing slightly, worried about his reaction.

"YES!" Harry bellowed, "this is just the best news ever! But how? I didn't think..." He trailed off, seeing Dionne's tentative smile.

"You're happy? Oh god, that's a relief, I was worried you might have thought I lied about the infertility." She exhaled a large breath that she hadn't realised she'd been holding.

"Happy? Try ecstatic. How did you find out?"

Lynne described the events of that afternoon to a grinning Harry. She had managed to persuade an obstetrician to work late, and fit them in for scans that evening. At least in America, money bought any service, any time.

Harry pulled Dionne up into his arms, and wrapped his arms around her as he kissed her. "This really is all my dreams coming true."

"You're my dream come true," said Dionne, welling up. "Now come on, we have to be at the hospital in half an hour."

CHAPTER 15

Harry held Dionne's hand while the doctor performed the scan. She pointed out a blob on the screen. "There we are, you're definitely pregnant. I'll measure the foetus, but it looks like you're about thirteen weeks, maybe fourteen. When was your last period?"

"Last October, but they've always been erratic," said Dionne, unable to take her eyes off the screen. *'Our baby'* she thought.

"Hmm, you may be even further along then. The pregnancy all looks fine, foetus looks as it should, but we can run more tests including a three D scan to make sure, given your age."

'We first slept together in November. Could it have been the first time?' Both had the same thought.

The doctor pressed a button to print out the scan, and handed it to Harry, who stared at the picture in amazement. She handed Dionne a paper towel to clean up, and turned to her computer.

"Measuring the foetus, it looks like you are nearer fifteen weeks." She handed Dionne some leaflets and a packet of pills. "Folic acid, start them today."

Dionne did a quick calculation, "I'm gonna be six months pregnant on our wedding day." She was horrified.

Harry just grinned, "who cares, you'll just be even more radiant."

"It's a bit chavvy, getting married six months pregnant."

"You're gonna look so cute being preggers, I really don't give a toss what anyone else thinks, besides, Lynne will be pregnant too." Harry pointed out, laughing.

They discussed the next steps with the doctor before wandering back to the waiting room hand in hand to wait for the others.

They sat in companionable silence for a little while, each absorbing the impact of the day's events.

Harry spoke first, "You really have changed my life you know. A few months ago, I would never have thought it possible for me to even have a regular girlfriend, let alone a wife, child and a sex life." He took a deep breath, "do you know what you mean to me, how much I love you?"

"Well a few months ago, I was a heartbroken widow, who thought I would spend the rest of my life pointlessly making money. I was lonely, full of regret, and hopeless. I never thought in my wildest dreams that you would appear, so yes, I think I share exactly the same feelings that you do."

"You're going to be a Mummy," said Harry, bumping shoulders with her. "You're gonna be a great mother, I just know it."

She grinned, "and you're gonna be a Daddy. What would you rather have, boy or girl?"

"Not fussed, what about you?" He said whilst daydreaming about a little girl wrapping her tiny arms round his neck.

Dionne sat and thought about it. "As long as it's got your genes, I don't care."

'Hmm, his looks, my brains, wow, this would be perfect. Better not say it though as he'll take the brains comment the wrong way' she thought.

Lynne and Dan were beaming when they returned to the waiting room hand in hand.

"So, how far gone are you?" Dionne asked.

"She thinks about four weeks," said Lynne, the grin not leaving her face. "What about you?"

"Fourteen or fifteen weeks. I think these two boys must be firing bullets to have got us both pregnant so fast," said Dionne, watching as both men puffed up slightly. They certainly both looked pretty pleased with themselves. "I'm going to be six months gone by the time we get married."

Lynne laughed. "How classy are we? They do maternity wedding dresses Di, so don't panic. I'm going to be almost four months gone, so I'll just look fat by then rather than pregnant."

They headed home to eat, as both women declared themselves 'starving'. Lynne pointing out that her lifelong diet was now officially over, and she wanted some chips.

That night in bed, Dionne lay awake pondering the pregnancy, when the thought hit her like a thunderbolt, *'I was drugged, what if it affected the baby?'*

She got up and padded down to her office. She sat and googled 'date rape drugs, the effects during pregnancy.' She read through all the articles listed on the first three pages of google, before being satisfied that there was unlikely to be any lasting damage, so she padded back to bed.

Harry woke up as she tried to sneak back in. "Everything alright?" He asked.

"I was worried about something, so I was down in my office looking on Internet."

Harry sat up. "What was you worried about?"

"The date rape drug, I was pregnant then, and I wanted to find out if there was likely to be any damage to the baby." She admitted.

Harry went cold. "What did you find out?"

"If it really was ketamine, which I think it was, given my symptoms, then it should have no effect on the foetus, given that it was just the once."

"Thank god for that, you should still discuss it with the doctor tomorrow though, put both our minds at rest," said Harry, pulling her into his favourite sleeping position. "Now try and sleep, you need your rest." She snuggled into his arms, and drifted off.

The next morning, Harry left Dionne asleep, creeping out of the bedroom as quietly as possible so as not to wake her. He sat in the kitchen to drink his coffee and eat his omelette before meeting Jack, his security, for the drive to work.

"I need to stop at a cashpoint on the way please Jack," said Harry. He was down to his last thirty dollars, and it was one of the cameramen's birthday the next day, so there was bound to be a whip round. They stopped at a bank, and Jack waited as Harry drew out five hundred dollars. He also pressed the button to get a balance on his account to check if the payment for Dionne's ring had been taken out ok.

Harry stared at the balance on the small slip of paper. He struggled to figure out the amount of zeros to work out the actual number. *'She only went and bloody did it, I thought she was joking.'*

"Everything all right sir?" Jack asked, seeing Harry frowning.

Harry stuffed the slip in his pocket. "Fine thanks." He pulled his phone out and text her.

you naughty girl, just seen my bank balance. You're not getting rid of me that easy ;)

Dionne smiled as she read the text shortly after waking up. She had wondered how long it would take him to discover his new billionaire status.

At latte o'clock she met Lynne by the pool. The agenda for the day was a doctors visit to check out the ketamine issue, which horrified Lynne when Dionne mentioned it, and discussions about their weekend away in St Lucia.

Lynne disappeared to pack, while Dionne made her way over to Dr Lucas' practice. He was one of the most exclusive doctors in Bel Air, and his luxurious consulting rooms reflected this. Dionne sat and told him exactly what had happened the night of the ball. He took her blood pressure, listened to her heart, and dished out lots of sympathy. He told her that it was highly unlikely the drug had harmed her foetus. Having seen her scan picture, he confirmed everything looked as it should. He took some blood for tests, and pencilled her in for a three D scan in a months time, generally reassuring her.

She stopped off at a bookstore on the way home, and bought a selection of books on pregnancy and childbirth to read during their weekend away. She still felt a bit dazed about the whole pregnancy issue, but reasoned it was just sheer luck that it had happened so quickly, as waiting wouldn't have been an option at her age.

'A husband and a baby, who'd have thought it?' She thought, smiling to herself.

She left a message on Harry's voicemail, giving him the good news from the doctor, and went home to join Lynne for lunch.

The men loved everything about the yacht. *'Boys and their toys'* thought Dionne, rolling her eyes at Harry and Dan checking out the Captain's bridge.

"So glad you got this Di, it's totally fantastic," exclaimed Harry, grinning. She grabbed his hand, and pulled him through the doorway to the accommodation below deck.

"Time for the guided tour," she laughed, "let me show you where we're sleeping."

Harry whistled through his teeth at the fabulous drawing room. "This is really quite something."

She showed him the study, spare bedrooms, and kitchen, before pulling him into the master bedroom. Harry surveyed the room, and checked out the ensuite.

"Through here," said Dionne, not sure how to handle showing him the nursery room. She unlocked the door, and stood aside to let Harry step inside.

Dionne watched his face to see his reaction. She was puzzled to find that he didn't react at all, just wandered around the room looking at the furnishings with what could only be described as a poker face.

"Don't you like it?" She asked him.

"I don't feel anything," said Harry rather cryptically as he wandered around, looking in the cupboards and the toybox.

"I thought this would be your thing."

"So did I. It feels like another life ago. Odd really."

'Why is this not exciting me?' He thought.

"The only way I can put this into words is that it's a bit like when I was scared of sex, it feels like a long time ago now. Wanting to be five again feels like a lifetime ago. I don't think I'm that man anymore. Am I making sense?"

"I think so. Or are you just saying this because I'm standing here?" Asked Dionne cautiously.

Harry shook his head, "I don't think so. I just don't feel like I want to sit and watch cartoons and retreat into my child state. Maybe it's because I'm gonna be a Father, I finally grew up." He kissed her forehead and walked back into the bedroom. Dionne followed him in and watched him nose through the drinks cabinet.

"Do you think this 'grown-out-of-it' thing is permanent? Or just temporary because of becoming a dad?"

Harry turned to look at her, "I have no idea, I just know that I have no desire to go back to my kid state right now. I've never lost the desire before, so I have no way of knowing if this is permanent or not. Tell you what," he took a deep breath, "I'll tell you first if I need it again."

Dionne smiled reassuringly, "ok, deal," as she pulled him into a hug.

"Come on, lets go find the others," said Harry, grasping her hand.

They found Lynne and Dan up on the deck. Lynne had her laptop out on the table in front of her. Harry fetched them all beers, and they settled onto the built in seating.

"This is the life," said Dionne lifting her face to the sun. "What are you looking at online?"

"This is my wedding planning file," said Lynne. "I thought with the four of us here together, it would be a good time to decide on all the plans. Harry did you find out about your nieces and nephew?"

"Yep, all three are extremely excited. I've done my guest list too, not many, but I don't have a huge family."

"Good. Is everyone ok with a cream and white theme?" They all nodded in agreement. "I thought tuxedos with cream dickies rather than morning suits, what do you two think?"

Both men nodded, rather relieved at not having to wear morning dress. "Bespoke or off the peg?" Dan asked.

"Bespoke, I spoke to Norton and Sons on Savile Row, and they are prepared to get your outfits made super fast. They are sending someone out to LA next week to measure you both. What about best men? Have you both decided? I need to organise their suits too."

"My eldest brother will be mine." Harry said.

"My cousin Joe has agreed to be mine." Dan added.

"I need their phone numbers to arrange appointments, plus numbers for the bridesmaid and pageboy's mothers so I can get them organised. Now that's settled, what about the first dance?" Lynne looked at them all expectantly. "One first dance for both couples or one each? Have you got a song?" She asked Dionne.

Dionne stole a glance at Harry. "Not as such, but songbird by Eva Cassidy holds happy memories for me."

Harry thought back to the wonderful night in Barbados when they both admitted they were in love, with that song as the soundtrack. "I love that song too, it should be our song really." He looked at Dionne with eyes full of love.

"Have you got a song?" Dionne asked Dan.

"Sex bomb," said Dan, making them all laugh.

"I think we'll go with Eva Cassidy," said Lynne, embarrassed.

With all the wedding decisions out of the way, the remainder of the weekend was spent exploring the island. Craig hired a car, and they spent the entire Saturday visiting beautiful deserted beaches, and the magnificent rain forest.

That night, they ate out at The Fox Grove Inn, enjoying the Creole food, and the magnificent view of the nearby Fregate Islands.

"This is truly paradise," said Harry, gazing out over the water.

"Reminds me of Barbados to be honest, if Barbados had a volcano, that is," said Dionne, scratching a gnat bite she picked up in the mangrove swamp.

CHAPTER 16

They returned to LA the following day. With both men working flat out to complete their filming commitments before the wedding, time off was strictly limited. Lynne was in her element dealing with party planners, dressmakers, and all the myriad details that make up an elegant, modern wedding. She commandeered the PA's old office, and threw herself into overseeing every detail. For the first time in her life, she was truly busy, and she loved it, gaining a sense of satisfaction that had always eluded her.

Dionne worked a little every day, keeping to her resolution to stop trading. All of her remaining investments were stable enough to be left alone, unless the guys needed her assistance for another 'project'. She spent the rest of her time reading all the pregnancy books from cover to cover, and organising her interior designer to add nurseries to all of her homes. She discovered that she enjoyed being pregnant, loved shopping for baby clothes, and life away from the screens was enormous fun.

Harry made the decision that his current film would be his last. Lorena's words regarding half a billion quid being enough for a lifetime, had made his mind up. Living in Dionne's world, where anonymity was king, meant that he was now viewing his fame as more of a nuisance than an advantage. Just the security arrangements for their wedding were a huge project, due to the media being obsessed with his and Dan's celebrity status.

With marriage and fatherhood ahead, Harry wanted to exit the world of crazy fans, Internet gossip pages and the intense scrutiny that a famous face brings. He just wanted to be a good husband, and a great

Dad.

Dan decided to be pickier about future roles. He swore never again to sign up for a film which required him to spend two hours every day getting into a ridiculous costume.

On a glorious day in May, two impossibly handsome men stood in a picturesque village church, waiting for their two brides to arrive. As the music started, they both turned to see two beautiful women walking up the aisle towards them, with a dapper, older man between them.

George had been delighted to have been asked to give them both away. Seeing Dionne and Lynne, both visibly pregnant, safely into the arms of their new husbands was a duty he took enormous pleasure in.

Harry gazed at Dionne in her wedding dress, which showed a reminder she was carrying his child, and made his heart leap with love.

As he slid the simple platinum band onto her finger, she looked up at the beautiful man, who she loved so totally, and sent up a silent prayer. *'Thank you John, for sending him, he's perfect in every way.'*

The End

ABOUT THE AUTHOR

D A Latham is a salon owner, mother of Persian cats, and devoted partner to the wonderful Allan.